Mencken and the Monsters

A Story of the Defense of Reality

Jeff Elkins

This book is a work of fiction. All the characters, organizations, and events portrayed in this novel are either products of the author's imagination or are used fictitiously.

ISBN: 1537379380
ISBN-13: 978-1537379388

DEDICATION

For my incredible wife, Wendy. I love you

ACKNOWLEDGMENTS

To my writing partner, Cory, all that planning is finally coming to life.

To my wonderful editors, Laura Humm and Everette Robertson without you this book would be unreadable. Thank you for all your hard work.

To my cover designer, Elizabeth Mackey, thank you for giving my words a face.

And finally, to my fantastic Beta Readers, Ann, Jenn, Kara, and Kim, this book is far better because you invested time in it. Thank you.

Baltimore
September 2015

CHAPTER ONE

"You're wasting your time. This story isn't going to save the city."

The smooth female voice tickled Mencken's ear, urging him to gaze on its beautiful source, but Mencken resisted the temptation to look up from his crouch. "What're you getting at?" he said, staring down at the black puddle of thick oil on the sidewalk in front of him.

"All I'm saying is that this is a waste of your time. There's nothing here. No story." The enchanting voice belonged to Detective Rosario Jimenez. Mencken knew that if he were to allow himself to look up, he would be trapped, able to do nothing but stare into her deep green eyes. He figured her hair was pulled back in a tight bun, leaving her perfect neck exposed. She was probably wearing those flawlessly fitting slacks and that blouse that always commanded his full attention.

He risked glancing at her shoes. They were white running shoes with pink laces. Just like her, strong and feminine, disarmingly beautiful, but able to run you down and kick your ass if you tried to bolt. This was why, Mencken knew, he could not look up. He could not break his focus, for if he gave Detective Jimenez the smallest amount of attention, she would bewitch him, and his day would be forsaken to dreams about her.

"Where you see nothing, I find truth," he said, working the oil-like substance between his fingers.

"You're so full of shit," she laughed.

Continuing to battle against her charms, he listened to her walk away. Mencken brought his fingers close to his face for a better look. The substance was sticky, but odorless. Mencken knew it was left over from the fight, but it didn't look like blood. He considered tasting it, but then stopped. Tasting strange substances found on the sidewalks of Baltimore was always a bad idea.

Mencken stood and looked down the street. The beat cops were wrapping up with the two witnesses. He moseyed in their direction, hoping the police would leave soon. He paused after ten yards and glanced back at the puddle. It sure looked like a pool of blood from afar. Sliding his arms out of the straps, Mencken shifted his backpack to his front. He unzipped the top and pulled the small notebook from inside. The notebook's black leather cover was worn and wrinkled. He removed the sharpened pencil from behind his ear and made a note about the location of the alleged crime.

Mencken watched as the boys-in-blue got in their cars and pulled away. The witnesses turned to leave. "Hey," Mencken shouted across the street. "Hey, hold up."

The two witnesses stopped and looked at him. The first was as fat as he was tall. He wore a loose-fitting white t-shirt and baggy jeans. A large, orange hair pick protruded from his perfectly rounded afro.

The second was a short, hard-looking, elderly man with a bald head, powerful forearms, squinty eyes, and slight under-bite. He had the smashed face of a boxer who'd never learned to duck. He wore gray sweats and a blue t-shirt with the Greek letters delta, sigma, and theta across the middle. Mencken doubted the old man had ever been to college. More likely, he'd picked the shirt up at the local

Goodwill.

"You guys got a second for the press," Mencken called as he drew closer.

The old man took a pack of cigarettes from the front pocket of his pants. He pulled a stick for himself with his teeth and then held the pack out for the fat man who accepted the cigarette, while producing a lighter from his pocket. Mencken smiled at the coordination. He respected strategic systems when he saw them. It was clear these unlikely partners were united for their mutual survival. The fat man flicked his lighter once with his thumb, then a second time, then rapidly over and over, but there was no spark.

Mencken reached into his pocket and retrieved a silver flip lighter. He didn't smoke. He carried it because lighting cigarettes for people tended to open them up.

"You don't look like press," the old man said, using Mencken's lighter to start his cigarette.

"Yeah," the fat man said, taking his turn with the lighter. "Yeah, you got a badge or something? Let us see your badge."

Mencken sighed. "Journalists don't have badges."

"Well," the fat man said, crossing his arms and tossing Mencken a suspicious look. "You got like a press pass, or credentials, or something?"

"What about a business card?" the old man said.

"Yeah. Yeah. We ain't saying nothing until you give us a business card," the fat man agreed.

Mencken reached into his right back pocket and removed his wallet. Digging through it he asked, "Why do you care? I just want to ask you what you saw." He passed the men two white cards. On each card there were only two words: Mencken Cassie. The men accepted the cards and examined them.

"Looks legit," the old man said.

"Alright," the fat man said, putting the card in his pocket. "Let's talk finder's fee."

Mencken sighed and looked into the sky. "You didn't find anything," he said.

"Listen up mother-fucker," the fat man said, pointing his finger in Mencken's face. "You've got to pay for my life story, because it's a fucking epic of giant proportions. This is Game of Thrones shit here. You got that. Sex. Drugs. Violence. Jail. Drugs. Lesbians. This story is huge, and if you're going to get famous off my shit, you've got to pay."

"Shut the fuck up," the old man said.

"What," the fat man replied, wounded. "I'm just trying to get us paid."

"I'm not paying you for anything," Mencken said.

"Come on, man," the fat man said. "Us brothers got to help each other out. Twenty bucks. Twenty bucks, and I'll tell you everything. Even the lesbian parts."

"Gentlemen, I don't have time for this," Mencken said, pulling his cell phone from his pocket to check the time. "Do you want to see your name in print or not?"

The two men looked at each other, confirmed, and then looked back at Mencken. "What do you want to know?" the old man said.

"Tell me what happened," Mencken replied.

"So here's how it went down," the fat man began, uncrossing his arms and waving them wildly. "Do you have like, a camera or something? Because you're going to want to tape this shit here."

"No. I don't have a camera. I'm a writer."

"Ooooh, big, tall, fancy man is a writer," the fat one mocked.

"Just get on with it," the older one said.

"Alright. Alright," the fat man said. "So we're coming out of a meeting."

"Are you a part of the Mission?" Mencken asked, nodding toward the old fire house behind them. The building served as a recovery center for homeless male addicts.

"Yeah, yeah. Afternoon meeting. It's the open one. Anyone can come in for lunch as long as they stay for the meeting. All kinds of weirdos come in off the street," the fat man explained. "So we was coming out of the meeting for a smoke, and there was this fish with us."

"Fish?" Mencken asked.

"Yeah, yeah. Fish. Like fresh fish. Like a new guy."

"Oh. Okay."

"So the fish was all asking us for a smoke, because we all need a little pick-me-up after Kevin shares. He talks about the most boring shit. Going on and on about how his grandmother died when he was just a kid. Oh it's so sad. My poor Mammy."

"Stick to the story," the old man grunted.

"Alright. Alright," the fat man said, frustrated at being reigned in. "So the fish was here and then the other two fish came up on us."

"Other two?" Mencken interrupted again.

"A man and a boy," the old man said.

"He wasn't a boy," the fat one said. "He was a like a teenager."

The old man snorted with indifference.

"So they came up on us," the fat man continued.

"Wait, wait," Mencken said. "Were they in the meeting?"

The two men looked at each other. "Why not?" the fat one said. "Sure. Yeah. They were in the meeting."

Mencken shook his head and looked at the sky again. It was getting dark.

"You want this story or not, cuz I can call other papers, you know. People going to compete for this," said the fat man, moving his hands down his body as if that was what was being sold.

"I'm sorry," Mencken said. "Continue."

"So they came up on us. And the fish was like, 'Just leave me be. I ain't done nothing.' And the other fish was like, 'You're here. That's enough.' And the first was all,

'Why you got to be like that? You don't have to do this. I'm not hurting anyone.' And then the teen was all, 'You ain't supposed to be on this side.'"

"This side?" Mencken asked.

"That's what he said," the old timer replied.

"And then the first fish was like, 'I'll leave. I'll get a coin and leave.'"

"Coin?"

"I don't know," the fat man said, angry at being interrupted again. "Maybe it was for the fucking bus. Do I look like a street interpreter or something? Zing-a-zang-a Whack-a Whack-a. That means 'let me finish my fucking story' in Street."

"Please, go on," Mencken said.

"So then the kid," the fat man said.

"You mean teen," the old man said with a grin.

"You mother-fucker," the fat man yelled. "Interrupt me again and see what happens. Just watch. I'll pound your old stupid ass."

The old man laughed.

"So the teen says, 'You don't have one. Even if you did, we couldn't let you use it.' Then the scary fish says, 'Enough talk. Finish it. But watch out for the tail.' Then the teen was like,"

"Watch the tail?" Mencken asked.

"Yeah," the fat man said. "That's what he said. 'Watch the tail.' You'd understand if you let me finish. Shit."

"I'm sorry," Mencken said again. "Go ahead."

"So he's all, 'Watch the tail.' And the kid does this roundhouse kick. Wham!" The fat man swung his foot in the air to demonstrate. "Then he punched the fish in the face. Za-cow!" The fat man swung wildly in the air with his right fist. "Then we was all like, ka-pow! And boom-boom!" the fat man exclaimed, kicking the air again with one foot and then the other. "And the fish was bleeding this black stuff all over the place. But then the fish, like, spun and lashed out with his tail." The fat man demonstrated, spinning in circles. "But the kid like, ran up his tail, using it like a step, and then he grabbed his chin, and snapped his neck. Wha-pow!" The fat man pantomimed snapping a man's neck with both hands. "And the fish went down. And all this black blood came out his mouth. But then the two fish grabbed the first fish's body, threw him in the trunk of the car, and drove off."

The fat man put his hands on his knees and sucked air in and out with desperation. "Phew," he said between breaths. "That's, um. That's how it happened."

"A tail?" Mencken replied.

"The cops didn't believe us either," the old man said.

Mencken looked over what he'd just jotted down in his notebook. "I don't know. A tail? You sure it wasn't, like, a crowbar or something? Maybe it just looked like a tail?"

"It was a mother-fucking, giant-ass, rat-looking tail, damn it. I said 'tail' and I meant a mother-fucking tail. So when you going to put us in the paper?" the fat man demanded.

"I don't think this one's going to make it to print," Mencken said, rubbing his shaved head with his right hand. "I don't think anyone is going to buy this karate-kid-versus-the-rat-man thing. But, I tell you what. I'll type it up and put it online."

"Teen," the old man said again, with a laugh.

"Fine, karate-teen-versus-the-rat-man," Mencken replied. "Like I said, no one's going to print it, but it should get some hits online. Can I use your names?"

"Sure," the old man said. "They call me Popeye."

"Of course they do," Mencken said, making a note in his book.

"And I'm Sexy Toni," the fat man said. "That's Sexy Toni with an 'i'."

"Where does the 'i' go?" Mencken asked.

"Where ever you want to stick it, baby," Toni said, with a seductive smile.

After thanking the two men, Mencken returned to his bike. He took the black helmet off the back, strapped it on, and swung his foot over the beast. He'd found the wrecked 2003 Dyna Super-Glide in the back of a used car lot ten years ago. It had taken him most of his junior year of high school to restore it. It was perfect for getting through the crowded streets of Baltimore. He revved the engine, soaking in the powerful growl of the monster.

Before pulling off, he glanced at his phone, thumbing through his Twitter feed.

@BmoreVoice, shots fired at harlem deli, monroe and harlem. no cops yet

That sounded promising, so Mencken returned the phone to his pocket and pulled onto the street in search of a real story.

CHAPTER TWO

Mencken pulled the heavy doors open with both hands. The glass of the doors and the four adjacent seven-foot windows was thick and textured, allowing pedestrians to see the presence of patrons without recognizing individuals. It was a perfect entrance to the double wide, three story rowhome that was Imani's Place.

Ignoring the "Please wait to be seated" sign, Mencken marched across the room and took up his normal table in the back, directly across from the doors. Five twenty-somethings lingered at the bar, laughing together. Of the twenty tables, only three were filled, each by a couple, eating and talking together. As always, Mencken took up residence in the chair with its back to the wall, giving him a full view of the space.

The restaurant sat in the midst of a residential block on the east side of the city. A hundred years ago, the place had been a famous haberdashery. For the past fifteen years, it had been owned and operated by the strong and beautiful Imani Douglas. That's how Mencken had described her in a review he once wrote for the City Paper, "strong and beautiful." Although she was only in her early thirties, Imani served as the unofficial matriarch of the community.

It was not unusual to see her counseling couples, giving career advice, or serving as a mediator in civic feuds.

In the morning, Imani ran her establishment as a coffee shop that served hot breakfast. The spot closed at eleven, and then reopened at three as a bar and grill. What made the restaurant especially unique was Imani's policy to never refuse anyone breakfast. Imani didn't care if her patron was homeless, or an addict who used all his last dollar on his last fix, or simply a freelance reporter scraping by with nothing; it didn't matter. Imani would give them a mug of coffee and something to eat. She simply ask that they pay when they were able. Socially conscious millennials loved the policy; often, they would pay for their meal twice so they could make a difference with their pancakes.

Mencken pulled his laptop from his backpack and opened the machine on the table. He glanced at the time in the bottom right corner. It read 7:20 pm. His first appointment would be there in ten minutes. He had two meetings lined up tonight. He thought of Imani's as his office. It was relatively quiet, close to his apartment, and well-known, even to those who didn't live on the east side. It helped that Imani didn't seem to care.

The restaurant's interior was simple. The walls were dark wood paneling on the bottom half and scarred drywall on top. The floors were unpolished hardwood. To Mencken's left was a long bar that ended in a cash register. Behind the bar was a large assortment of drinks and a big, black griddle. Imani's cuisine wasn't fancy. If it couldn't be made on the griddle or in the deep fryer, then she didn't serve it. The only strange addition was the large, wooden circle that hung above the bar. Measuring four feet in diameter, it was cracked and old. Carved into the middle was a large lower case "g" with the word "home" underneath. When asked, Imani would simply explain that it was a family heirloom.

Mencken opened his browser, logged into his blog, and looked at his stats. His afternoon post, "Popeye, Sexy

Toni, and the Lizard Man" received 135,000 hits. He tried to calculate in his head how many advertising dollars that would pull from the ads that ran next to the story, but math had never been his thing.

"Always with your face in the computer," Imani said, placing a heavy, glass beer mug in front of Mencken. She took the seat across from him, leaned back in her chair, and stretched her arms out across two chairs from the empty table behind her. Her biceps were lean and defined. She wore a black tank top over a gray tank top and camouflaged cargo pants. The outfit in combination with her super-cropped afro and captivating brown eyes gave her the look of a warrior princess.

"You look ready for battle," Mencken said, peaking up from his laptop.

She laughed and teased, "Every day's a struggle, until you come in the room."

Mencken took a sip of the beer. It was light, but had bite. "I'll be able to pay you in about an hour," he said, putting the mug back down.

"You know family eats free," she said.

Mencken snorted at the word "family." She knew barely anything about him. Sure, he used this back table as his office every night, and yes, he'd been doing so for at least two years, but what did she know about him? If the shoes were switched, he wouldn't be handing her free beers.

She leaned forward, resting her elbows on her knees. "You catch any big stories today?" she asked.

"Not really," he replied as he wrote a reply to an email.

"Come on," she said, pushing his knee. "I'm trapped in this place all day. I don't get to see anything fun. Spill." Mencken knew Imani wasn't exaggerating. She lived in the third-floor apartment above the restaurant. She usually worked both breakfast and dinner. He suspected the only time she left the place was to go shopping during the lunch break.

Mencken sighed and looked up from the screen. "There was a robbery over in Sandtown today."

"Boring," she said. "When is there not a robbery in Sandtown?"

Mencken grimaced. It was okay if he called his stories mundane, but not if someone else did. He looked back at his laptop, opening the articles he'd written recently. "Oh, here's one you'll like," he said, stumbling on a quirky story he'd written last night.

Imani cocked her head and smile with anticipation.

"The city fined a man in Belair Edison for keeping an illegal number of cats in his house. Something about that many cats being a health hazard."

"How many cats does it take to rack up a felony?" she asked, intrigued.

"Not sure. But he had over four hundred living with him in his two story home."

"Oh shit," Imani exclaimed.

"You better believe it. Everywhere," Mencken teased.

"You dig anymore into your Cabal theory?" she asked with genuine interest.

Mencken was put off by the word "theory." It wasn't a theory. It was real, and he was going to prove it. Whenever she asked, he regretted letting her in on his secret. He'd had too many free beers and had become too loose-lipped. He wished she'd forget he'd ever said anything. "Nothing I'm willing to share," he said, going back to his email.

"Alright," she laughed, standing. "I get it. I get it. You need to keep your cards close to your vest." Before returning to the bar she added, "If you want any food, just wave. We'll hook you up."

"Thanks," Mencken replied, but he didn't plan to stay long enough to eat.

As Imani walked away, the front door swung open. In walked Richard Winchell, a short, round man in his early sixty. He wore a rumpled, brown suit, with an unmemorable tie, and horn-rimmed glasses that looked like they'd been teleported onto his face from the 1950s. Winchell wanted nothing more in life than to retire, but his divorce left him financially strapped. He often joked that he would drop dead at the paper. He was the senior editor of the Baltimore Star. Once upon a time, the title carried weight and glamour. Now it was little more than a reminder of what the industry use to be.

The Star had been racked by waves of layoffs as subscriptions continually decreased. Winchell hated turning to freelancers like Mencken. He longed for the old days when the news room was full of Menckens, all chasing the next story, all competing for the front page byline. Now the crime desk consisted of two reporters.

Winchell made his way across the room to Mencken's usual spot. He took his coat off and sat down across from Mencken. "Alright kid," Winchell said in his grumbling, don't-waste-my-time voice. "What do you have for me?"

Mencken closed his laptop. "I got a seven-hundred word interview with the shop owner who was robbed at gun point in Sandtown this morning. I've got a fifteen-hundred word write up of the shooting last night outside the Hopkins Homewood campus, including quotes about 'safety' from bystanders. And I've got a three thousand word piece on the skyrocketing murder rate, correlating the rise in violent crime with the decreased police presence in impoverished neighborhoods." Mencken leaned back and interlocked his fingers behind his head.

"You got a City Hall source on the correlation?"

"Not a source, per se," Mencken said.

"You at least got a quote? Don't tell me you're just making crap up now." Winchell looked at his wristwatch and yawned.

"I've got a cop confirming they've decreased their presence in rougher neighborhoods since the riots." It had been a difficult six months for Baltimore. The mayor claimed the riots would relieve tension and that the city would go back to normal. It hadn't. As the police had grown gun-shy, gangs had started to vie for power in the streets, causing the number of violent crimes and the murder rate to skyrocket.

Winchell crossed his arms with suspicion. "Cop let you use his name?"

"No," Mencken said, with frustration. "But the quote's real."

"Fine. Email me two and three. I'll run them tomorrow."

"What about the robbery?"

"Listen kid, no one cares about a liquor store in a horrible neighborhood being robbed. It's like saying, 'Teenage girl has bad attitude.' Or 'Stupid cat videos go viral on the internet.' Or, 'In face of crisis, City Council doesn't do shit.' It's not news, kid."

Mencken looked down at his lap. He wouldn't admit it, but he longed for Winchell's approval. In his day, Winchell had been a force to be reckoned with. His investigative work had brought down city council members. He'd exposed the misuse of campaign funds by a mayoral candidate. He'd uncovered a conspiracy in the 80s to keep African Americans from buying houses in an affluent neighborhood. A series he'd written on immigrants in Baltimore had even been nominated for a Pulitzer.

Winchell slid two envelopes across the table. "Normal rate?" he said.

Mencken took the envelopes and thumbed through the cash. It wasn't much, but it was something. "Looks good," he said.

"Alright," Winchell said standing. "Email me tomorrow by six if you've got anything else worth reading."

"Will do," Mencken said.

Winchell stood to leave. "Keep at it, kid," he said. "You'll break something big eventually. It's just about time and patience."

Mencken watched him leave with admiration. Although he'd never admit it out loud, Winchell was the type of old-world journalist Mencken hoped to become.

Mencken waved to Imani. Seconds later a plate of fries was delivered by a short, thin twenty-something in a Pacman t-shirt. Mencken took a bite. They were crisp and seasoned with Old Bay and vinegar, just like he liked them.

The door opened again. Mencken's second appointment had arrived. More professional looking than Winchell, Sam Dandrip was a radio show host, podcaster, columnist for the Star, and figurehead of the Baltimore Magazine – a monthly publication that confused Mencken. Copies of it were everywhere, but he'd never actually seen anyone reading it. He wasn't sure how the journal kept going, much less how they paid writers like Sam.

"Damn it. Not elbow patches," Mencken mumbled under his breath as Sam approached. Tonight Sam was dressed in pressed blue jeans, gleaming-white tennis shoes, a blue button down, and a brown sport coat with patches on the elbows. The pretension of the patches made Mencken's head pound.

Unlike Winchell, Mencken had little respect for Sam. The man was a decent enough writer, and he worked hard – hard enough, anyway. But Mencken didn't see anything extraordinary. Rather, Mencken believed Sam had simply been in the right place at the right time. Sam had come along at the climax of the newspaper age. He'd gotten a job as a columnist at a time when they were handing those positions to whomever wanted one. He'd started a radio show after others had paved the way, and now that podcasting was booming, he was jumping onboard. Sam was the opposite of an early adopter. He consistently rode the final wave, coasting through right before the door of opportunity was slammed shut.

"Mr. Cassie," Sam said, taking the seat across from Mencken and extending his hand.

"Mr. Dandrip," Mencken said, returning the gesture. The two men shook.

Sam motioned at the bar for a waitress. "What do you

have for me this week?" he said with a smile.

Imani arrived at the table with a light colored local beer in a frosty mug and a plate of cheese fries. "How are you tonight, Sam?" she said, placing the food in front of him.

"You are God's gift," he said to her with a smile. "I mean it. You are the absolute best. All the people coming in and out of here, and you remember my order. Thank you."

Mencken snorted at Sam's overly genuine tone.

"Thank you, Sam," Imani replied, shooting a glare at Mencken. "It's nice to be appreciated."

The only son of a surgeon and a news anchor, Sam had gone to the best high schools, which in turn had propelled him to an Ivy League university. He had started at the news desk at the Star because a university professor who enjoyed Sam's humor in class had friends at the paper. After a few years, Sam had been given his own column because he was safe. He never took risks. He never offended. He never stood out. He kept it all vanilla, and in a world of chaos, vanilla is comforting. In the wake of Rush Limbaugh's rise to glory, Sam had been offered a day time talk show on the local NPR station, to bring moderate balance to the conservative hurricane.

Mencken could not be more different. The third son of divorced parents, raised by a single mom who worked late shifts as a nurse, Mencken had fought and scrapped for every inch of success. It had taken him six years to graduate from the University of Maryland, Baltimore County, because working full time had kept him from taking full class loads. When he had finally received an English degree, he'd spent a month looking for a newspaper job, but there were none to be had. They were already filled by the Sams of the world.

Mencken had saved money living in his mother's basement. By day, he had worked minimum wage jobs. At night, he had built a following of devoted Baltimore readers, giving them insights and stories the established papers deemed too risky to print. When he could, he'd sell a piece of writing here or there. At first, seeing his name in print had been a thrill, but soon he'd grown to realize that what the local news organizations were really buying was his reputation. His readers were more loyal than theirs. When they ran his stuff, his readers showed up. Mencken didn't resent this; rather, he saw it as a strategic solution.

"Let's get this done," Mencken said as Imani left. "I've got five for you this week."

Sam pulled a gooey fry from the mound, stretching out the cheese until it broke. He held it high above his head, letting the long string of cheese enter his mouth first, then consuming the fry. "Have you had these? You really need to try them," Sam said as he chewed. "Seriously, I'm not going to eat them all."

Sam made this same offer every week. Each time he made it, it was as if he were making it for the first time. It was another thing about meeting with Sam that drove Mencken insane with frustration. "No. Thank you. I'm fine," Mencken said. "So, five stories for you this week."

Sam repeated the action with another fry and then took a long swig of the beer. "Okay," he said. "I'm ready. Hit me with them."

Putting respect to the side, Mencken's relationship with Sam was different than his relationship with Winchell. Sam never put Mencken's name on anything. Mencken was Tabasco. If applied directly to Sam's empire, Sam's vanilla-loving followers would fall away.

Rather, Sam paid for Mencken's eyes and ears on the street. Sam was thought to be "a man of the city," that's what his marketing campaigns said anyway. Unfortunately for his publicist, Sam hadn't lived in the city for nearly two decades. He owned a small farm forty minutes north of the beltway on the Mason-Dixon Line. The rustic homestead was complete with a large garden, horses, and chickens. To maintain his authentic connection to the city, Sam paid Mencken. Mencken gave Sam stories. Sam rewrote them in his own voice or shared them on his podcast.

Mencken began running through the stories he'd prepared. "Over in Locust Point, a one-hundred-and-two-year-old woman has a birthday next week. I've got a four thousand word interview with her. And yes, she said she'd be open to come on the radio show if you want her. She's a big fan."

Sam smacked the table with excitement. "Wow, a hundred-and-two? What is that? Nineteen? Um. Nineteen-ten? Nineteen-twelve?"

"She was born November second, nineteen-thirteen," Mencken corrected.

Sam ate another fry. "Both World Wars. The Depression. McCarthy. Kennedy. I bet she can talk about all of it. How sharp is she?"

"She's pretty sharp," Mencken said, checking the time on his cell phone. He didn't have anywhere to be; he was just curious at how much time had passed. "She's more interested in talking about how Locust Point used to be all white."

Sam laughed, took another drink, and stuffed a mound of fries in his mouth. "Old people, right?" he said with a full mouth. "That sounds amazing. Good work."

To his credit, for the two years they'd been doing this dance, Sam had never plagiarized Mencken. He always rewrote Mencken's work in his own voice, adding his own moderate political thoughts when he could. If he told a story on the radio, he would quote an "unnamed source." Occasionally, he'd even refer to Mencken as "a member of my team." Mencken knew Sam didn't have to do that. He'd paid for the stories. Mencken had signed a non-disclosure agreement. Sam could take the stories and pretend Mencken never existed, if Sam wanted. Mencken appreciated the man's integrity. Sam wasn't going to take credit for something that wasn't at least partially his.

"Second story," Mencken said, moving on, "is a pair of

twins in Towson. They both play tennis – doubles. They've received scholarships to the University of Maryland. I wrote it up in fifteen-hundred words."

"Awesome," Sam said. "Perfect for the show. Great stuff."

"Next," Mencken said, looking at his laptop for a refresher, "I've got an interview with a couple that just opened an organic market in Hampden. They only sell locally sourced produce."

"Ooo," Sam cooed, eating more fries. "That sounds great. How long?"

"About three thousand words."

"That's perfect. I'll use it as the basis for the column next week. People are really hungry for stories like that." Sam smiled and nodded, waiting for Mencken to acknowledge the pun.

Mencken didn't respond.

"Come on," Sam pleaded. "Hungry? They're hungry for the organic food. Huh? Huh? It's funny." Sam took another drink. "You play it cool, but I know you're laughing on the inside."

"I've got a story on the sixth graders from City Neighbors Charter School. They did a reenactment of a sit-in at a pharmacy on Lexington Street."

"Read's Drug Store?" Sam replied, seriously. "Nineteen-fifty-five. That maybe the column. That's important history. Great work snagging that story. I don't know how you find all of these. What do you think? Is this a radio piece or a column?"

"The teacher said he'd bring some of the kids on your show to talk about the experience, so I'd go with radio. Here's his number." Mencken pulled a business card from his backpack and passed it across the table.

"Excellent," Sam said, putting the card in his wallet.

"The last one is a three thousand word piece on the arrival of tiramisu in the States. First place to serve it in the US was a small restaurant in Little Italy in the sixties,"

Mencken continued.

"Is that true?" Sam said. He swirled a fry in the grease pooling on the plate and then popped the fry in his mouth.

"Seems to be," Mencken said. "One of the pastry chefs over a Vaccaro's makes a strong case for it."

Sam finished his beer in a final swig. Wiping his mouth with his sleeve and then smacking his knees with both hands, he said, "You know, I only really need four, but all five of these sound amazing. And I know your background work is impeccable. I'll take all five. We'll use all of them somewhere. Thank you so much. You do such great work. I'm amazed. Truly. Amazed."

Mencken took a final drink of his beer and started packing up his laptop.

"Standard rate per piece?" Sam said with a smile.

"Sounds good," Mencken replied. He stood and stretched.

Sam removed a checkbook from the inside of his coat. As he wrote out the check, he asked, "So how is your mom? Is she still taking shifts at Hopkins?"

"Yep," Mencken replied, impatiently tapping his foot.

"That's great. To raise someone as talented as you, she must be really special." Sam tore out the check and handed it over.

"Thanks," Mencken said, taking the check, reading it, and sticking it in his back pocket.

"Same time and place next week?" Sam asked with a smile.

"Sounds good," Mencken said.

"Same bat time. Same bat channel," Sam said to himself with a grin.

Mencken gave a half-hearted nod and headed for the door. On the way out he waved to Imani.

"See you tomorrow," she called after him.

CHAPTER THREE

In the mist outside of Imani's. Mencken allowed the wet breeze to wash his face. It had been an unusually warm September. The damp cold snapped at his throat, sending a spark down his spine, renewing his energy.

Mencken crossed the street, turned the corner, and unlocked the door on the side of a corner rowhome. He stepped inside the small entry hall and glanced at the thin, black mail box on the wall with his last name written in white chalk. It looked empty. He decided not to check. Instead, he climbed the stairs to the third floor and unlocked his door.

His apartment consisted of one room. To the far left of the front door was a white sink framed by brown wooden cabinets. The countertops were faded green and covered in knife scars from decades of tenants use. Past the kitchen was a bathroom with a standing shower. To the right, against the wall, was a single bed. There was no frame, just a box spring and a mattress. A folding chair and card table dominated the center of the room. The flimsy table was littered with art supplies. But a stranger visiting Mencken's apartment for the first time would miss all of these things because everything in the apartment was overshadowed by the wall across from the front the door.

The white wall had a floor-to-ceiling map of Baltimore drawn on it. Mencken had painstakingly traced the map on the wall with various colored Sharpies, an old overhead projector, and transparencies printed from Google maps. Covering the map were multi-colored Post-It notes. In Mencken's system, there were three different colors of notes, each with a specific meaning. Blue notes were events or crimes which Mencken felt bore no relation to his larger investigation. They were scattered all over the map. The Yellow post-it notes were for events or crimes Mencken suspected might be connected. These also were spread out all over the map.

The red notes were the important ones. These were the ones, Mencken believed without a shadow of a doubt, were directly connected to his investigation. These notes were concentrated in five areas: the south Baltimore peninsula, where the wealthy people lived; the northeast corner of the city, where suburbia and the city blurred; a strip down the middle of the city following North Avenue; a spattering on the northwest side of the city; and a large grouping by the waterfront on the southeast side of the city.

Mencken sat down in the chair, removed his notebook from his backpack, and began making new post-it notes. A high-school kid shooting at another on the west side was blue – a natural byproduct of generational poverty and teenage hormones.

The finalization of an elementary school closure in a northern neighborhood – again blue. At the Royal Farms store down the street from the school, Mencken had been told by the cashier that the school's administration had been underperforming for over a decade.

The purchase of three rowhomes just north of Johns Hopkins Hospital by the Baltimore Development Corporation got a yellow post-it. Why those three houses? They'd been abandon for years Residents were fleeing that neighborhood, not seeking to move in. Was the purchase some kind of favor to a city council member? Was the Baltimore Development Corporation planning some kind of crazy new construction there? Or, as Mencken really suspected, were the houses purchased by the Cabal to ensure they would stay vacant, so the property values would not improve, putting pressure on city council members so they could be challenged in the next election?

Mencken stood and secured the first three Post-It notes on the wall with thumbtacks. He had close to thirty more to finish before he would allow himself to sleep. After securing the notes, he turned to face the opposing wall. To the right of the door, three years ago, Mencken had used drywall glue and massive sheets of porcelain steel to create a large, floor-to-ceiling whiteboard.

When Mencken had begun to suspect that factions in the city who shouldn't work together were moving in orchestrated harmony to produce profitable outcomes. A street gang would increase drug sales in a neighborhood, causing an increase in crime. As housing prices plummeted, and the number of vacants skyrocketed, one of many legitimate development corporations would sweep in and start grabbing all the cheap real estate. At some point, a switch would flip and the police would increase their presence. Crime statistics in the neighborhood would drop as gangs moved on to another section of town. At the same time, the elementary school would be awarded a game-changing grant by a philanthropic organization. Then in unison newly renovated houses would hit the market for purchase or rent, and retail organizations would announce their intention to establish a renewed presence in the neighborhood. Then, often, there was a new contender for the city council member of that district, or a neighborhood meeting would be held at which people would demand millions of dollars in infrastructure improvements, or public transportation was rearranged to accommodate the growth and millions in contracts went to subcontractors to handle the increase in travel.

Mencken had tracked the cycle nine times in the past five years. The chess games took years to unfold and ran concurrently. Sometimes they encompassed a few blocks. Other times it led to major public works projects that spanned the city. Mencken was certain that was where the real money was – state-funded public works projects. It always seemed to be the end goal. Money would pour in, and while some of it would sprinkle over its target, much of it seemed to leak down unseen gutters.

The mystery that currently eluded Mencken was: who had the power to orchestrate all the needed moving pieces? Was there a single mastermind, or a committee of gang leaders, or was it just rich guys on their roof decks plotting world domination over cigars and brandy? Mencken had begun to sketch it out on the homemade whiteboard glued to the wall. He called the invisible hierarchy "the Cabal." He knew that without proof of these power holders, there was no story, there was only speculation and explainable trends.

At the bottom left of the whiteboard were the names, and occasionally pictures, of gang leaders. Each was marked with the name of the gang they oversaw and the neighborhood where they were based. If Mencken didn't have the leader, he had the name of the gang with a question mark over it. Next to the gangs were the crooked cops. The more senior the officer, the higher they were on the wall. Next to the cops were politicians and bureaucrats who were on the take. A few years ago, Mencken had been looking into the finances of lifelong City Hall workers – those middle managers that stayed when administrations changed. He found several with nicer houses and cars than they should have. Following campaign donations, Mencken had found that nine of the fifteen city council members were almost entirely funded by the three Baltimore-based development companies: Baltimore Development Incorporated, Rebuild Baltimore, and the

Gilford Development Corporation. Mencken was increasingly becoming convinced that the mayor was paid as well, but he couldn't prove it yet, so her name wasn't on the wall.

Above these three groups were the names, occupations, and pictures of the people he believed were either sitting at the table of power or close to it. There was an old gangster who went by the title "Agamemnon." He lived in a nice suburban neighborhood west of the city and had managed to remain untouchable for over a decade. There were also the heads of the three major Baltimore-based development firms. These CEOs stood to earn more from the Cabal than anyone else. And a certain hotel owner who was also the primary investor in the new Harrah's casino recently constructed on the southwest side of downtown. Mencken suspected he was a new player in the game.

Above these names, at the very top of the board, were two question marks. Mencken didn't believe any of the names and faces on the board had the drive or patience to organize a system of power so massive and secret. They were all too public, too polished, too easy to find. He believed there had to be someone else. Someone with his or her feet in both the business and criminal worlds – a boss. The first question mark was for the boss.

The second question mark was new. Within the past year, two community organizers had disappeared, a city council member had been killed in a hit-and-run, and a lawyer who'd been chasing members of the Cabal for fraud had been gunned down in the Inner Harbor. These crimes were too perfect, too precise. Under the question mark, Mencken had written the word "Hitman?" He felt absurd every time he looked at it, but he couldn't put the pieces together in his head without a professional killer in the mix. Gangs and thugs just couldn't pull off the things the Cabal needed.

Mencken's eyes ran over the board. There were lots of holes. He still didn't understand how the whole system held together, how they communicated, or what their end goal was. There was so much he didn't understand. Did they have meetings? Were they even aware of each other? Or were they all just minions of the question mark at the top? He just didn't know - yet.

There were footsteps on the stairs. Mencken immediately knew who it was. His downstairs neighbor came up to try and distract him at least three nights a week. He considered turning the lights out and pretending he wasn't home, but he knew it wouldn't do any good. If she wanted to come in, she was coming in. Mencken turned his chair to face the door and sat down to wait.

The footsteps came to a stop in front of his door. He watched his door knob jiggle, then, the lock turned, and the door opened. Detective Rosario Jimenez stepped into the room. Her soft brown hair was pulled back in a pony-tail. She wore loose-fitting gray sweats, yellow flip flops, and a forest green t-shirt that made her emerald eyes glow. She smiled, and Mencken's heart stopped, but his exterior remained stoic.

"You need to stop picking my lock. You do know it's against the law, right?" Mencken said, his arms crossed in defensive disapproval. "I should call the cops and have you arrested."

Rosie smiled. "Go ahead. Call 9-1-1. See how that works out for ya," she said as she walked over to his sink, opened the cabinet on the left, and took out a dusty glass. She cleaned the inside of it with the bottom of her t-shirt. "Oh, when you call, ask for Robert and Owen. Owen owes me ten bucks. The dummy can't help but bet on the Ravens, doesn't matter how bad they look. Also, I bet he'd love to see the picture you have of him on the bottom of your wall-o-evil over there." She motioned to the whiteboard with her head, and then inspected the inside of the glass. Satisfied, she filled the glass with water from the tap.

Mencken turned his chair around and started working

on another post-it. "I'm busy. What do you need?" he said, his head buried in his journal. There was nothing more he wanted than to give into whatever whim had brought her over, but he couldn't afford the distraction. He needed to finish this. The city needed him to finish it. The Cabal didn't rest, so neither could he.

Rosie sat on the floor next to him, looking up at the map on the wall. "Did you get the robbery in Roland Park?" she said, reaching up and stealing a pen from the table.

Mencken sighed. "That was yesterday," he said, not looking up from his journal.

"Give me a yellow," she said.

He looked at her with a belittling stare.

"Please," she said. "As if your little art project here is so hard to figure out." She reached up and grabbed one of the yellow pads. After a few seconds of scribbling, she put the note in the left center, a few blocks west of a blue one. "There was a second break-in today. Broad daylight. A moving truck backed up to a lawyer's front door. Clean the entire house out and drove off."

"I don't know," Mencken said. "I get that there are two, but what's so important about Roland Park? It should be blue. Blue is just regular crime."

"I know what blue is," she said raising an eyebrow at him.

In truth, although Mencken would never admit it, about a third of the notes on the wall were hers. She'd been doing this dance with him for almost a year now. He knew it frustrated her that he still treated her like an outsider. He wished he had the time a woman of her caliber deserved, but he didn't. His mission came first.

"This one's not about where, it's about who," she continued. "Both houses belong to lawyers at the firm of Dalton and Dalton."

Mencken looked at the ceiling. The name was there, in his head, somewhere. He just couldn't land it.

"Should I wait for you to get there on your own," she said with a grin.

"Just tell me," he replied, flipping through his notebook.

"Dalton and Dalton is the firm commissioned by the governor to look into the legal ramifications of adding to the subway system."

"I knew I knew that name," Mencken said.

Rosie looked at the wall again. "I bet the robberies weren't about money. I bet they were looking for something on the subway system."

Mencken nodded, seeing it now. "Yeah," he said. "Maybe."

Rosie shook her head and rubbed her forehead in exasperation. Then she turned to face him.

Mencken swallowed. Fighting back the urge to be overcome by her beauty.

"So what do you say you give this a thirty-minute break? I made tamales and rice. I've got a plate downstairs with your name on it."

"I can't," he said, looking back into his book.

She sighed. "You know both my parents were Mexican, right? So when I say I made tamales, I'm not talking about some frozen, prepackaged shit. I'm saying I made tamales."

Mencken's heart screamed from inside his chest, demanding he follow the amazing woman, the perfect woman, his perfect woman downstairs to her apartment, but his mind silenced the cry. There was work to do. He refused to look up from his journal. "I can't," he said. "Sorry."

"Fine," she snapped back. "Fine." She marched toward the door. Grabbing the handle, she turned and said, "I'll just go find someone else to share my tamales with." She slammed the door so hard, the post-its on the opposing wall shook.

Mencken listened to her storm down the stairs. He

heard her door slam. He breathed deeply, calming the fire of regret raging in his stomach. He looked back at the wall, then down at his notebook. Closing his eyes, he breathed deeply a second time, and then he went back to work.

CHAPTER FOUR

"What has been accomplished here is a remarkable phenomenon," Michelle Drake said with pride. The District Five City Councilwoman stood on a makeshift platform and spoke through a megaphone to a crowd of neighborhood residents and members of the press. The red, shiny megaphone was her trademark. It went with her to every public appearance, even if the appearance was indoors and the megaphone was unnecessary. It was a callback to her start in politics when she, a lowly Morgan State student, had led a protest at a school board hearing. When the board had moved into a closed-door session, she had taken up a bullhorn in the lobby. The elementary school on the chopping block was saved, and the political career of Michelle Drake had begun.

"These residents have taken a dilapidated representation of malfunction in our city, and made the dying domiciles a symbol of the vivaciousness of which we are capable," Drake said. She wore a red Under Armour running suit that matched her megaphone.

"They have taken something uncultivatable, something uninhabitable, something unprofitable, a pestilence on our polis, and they have resuscitated it, revitalizing the temperament of our citizenry."

Even though the neighborhood residents didn't fully follow the speech, they clapped in appreciation when she paused.

The effort had been remarkable. Residents of the Pimlico neighborhood had taken it upon themselves to demolish two abandoned homes, dispose of the rubble, and turn the double-wide, empty lot into a free community garden. The work had taken four months. No city funds had come to their aid. No outspoken politicians had called for demolition. No one outside of the neighborhood had known the project was happening until it was done. But now that it was done, Michelle Drake wasn't going to miss the opportunity to capitalize on the work.

"This paragon must be perpetuated," Councilwoman Drake continued. "It is an illustration that must be drawn again and again. This is what happens when assiduous citizens come together to build a commendable society. It was not our ineffectual State Representatives in Annapolis who did this. It was not our lethargic governor who did this. It was not even our unindustrious mayor. No. This splendiferous farm isn't the work of the legislature. It's the work of our neighborhood, the work of our hands, and the city must diagnosticate their disease in contrast."

The crowd clapped again.

"Now, I will be taking questions from members of the press," Councilwoman Drake said. "So ask away."

Hands shot up throughout the audience.

"Yes, you sir," the councilwoman said, pointing.

"Hello ma'am," a well-dressed reporter said. She had a large microphone in her hand, and a cameraman at her side. "I'm Cheryl Madden, WBAN-TV. What kind of crops will be grown on this farm? And who will be responsible for the upkeep?"

"Well, now," Councilwoman Drake said with a smile. "Why don't I bring the farmer himself up? Bill? Where's Bill?" she said scanning the crowd. "Bill. Bill Moss. Come on up here."

A short, but large-shouldered man in jeans and a black t-shirt stepped toward the platform. He walked with his head down. He was bald, with a thick mustache. Mencken guessed he was in his mid-fifties, but it was hard to tell.

"This, everyone, is Bill Moss. Bill is the virtuosic facilitator behind this unprecedented effort," the councilwoman said. Bill waved to the crowd. Neighbors cheered.

Cheryl Madden jumped in. "Mr. Moss, how did you get this idea to farm the land? And what do you plan to grow?"

Michelle motioned for Bill to speak. The older man cleared throat and said, "Well, my, um, my family sent me to a rehab facility in upstate New York."

He was difficult to hear without the megaphone. The crowd pressed in. An unnamed woman yelled, "We love you, Bill!"

Bill looked up and smiled. "Anyhow, um, while I was there I got my shit together. I'm sorry. I shouldn't say shit. I, um, I got my stuff together, and I learned a few things. I, um. I always liked planting stuff. Even as a kid. So when I came back, this here just made sense to me. I mean, those houses been vacant since I left. Nobody wanted 'em."

"And that's how neighborhoods metamorphize," Councilwoman Drake interrupted with her megaphone. Bill winced at its volume so close to his ear. "Bill here is a paladin, an exemplar, a champion of our metropolis."

"Excuse me," a man in a suit said. He also held a microphone in his right hand and had a camera man on his hip. "I'm Ernest Cartwright of WJY Morning Edition. Mr. Moss, will spaces on the land be leased to individuals? Or will people in the neighborhood buy shares of the produce?"

"I, um," Bill stumbled. "I just figured we'd start with some simple stuff? Maybe some tomatoes and zucchini? It's a good spot for tomatoes. And I just figured I'd grow 'em. Whoever wants 'em can come and pick 'em. As long as they don't go to waste.

"And that," the Councilwoman interrupted again with her megaphone, "is the epitome of authentic earnestness."

"Excuse me," Mencken called from the center of the crowd. "Mencken Cassie, The Baltimore Star, here. Ms. Drake, isn't it true that the two lots in question are owned by the Gilford Development Corporation? As this neighborhood's councilwoman, have you made arrangements with them to protect this land from development?"

"While I don't personally associate with persons at the Gilford Development Corporation," the councilwoman replied, "I've been assured that they are planning to maintain the site for the farm. Are there any other questions?"

"Ms. Councilwoman," Mencken yelled. "One more question, please. I find it odd that you say you don't know anyone at Gilford Development since their COO was your largest campaign donor in the last election. Will he also be supporting your run for mayor in two-thousand-sixteen?"

"Mayor, well, I don't know about that," she said through her megaphone, feigning embarrassment. "I try not to give credence to donators. It makes me less susceptible to lobbying interests and corruption."

"Very admirable Ms. Councilwoman," Mencken shouted. "In that spirit of transparency, I'd like for you to address the paper I obtained from the city permits office. It's a permit for construction on this site for a convenience store."

"I'm not sure what you are referring to, sir," the Councilwoman said, still through her megaphone. "Now if there are any other questions, I think we've-"

"Ms. Councilwoman, I have another question." The blue megaphone Mencken held increased the initial volume of his voice tenfold. "I have it on good authority that at the last council meeting, four days ago, you supported the rezoning of these two lots from residential to commercial properties. If ma'am, it is as you say, and you do not know the owners of these lots at Gilford Development-"

"I won't stand for these slanderous insinuations! This is nonsense! Pure nonsense!" the councilwoman yelled through her megaphone.

Mencken yelled back through his own, "If you do not know them, and this community farm is to be free, why then are you having the rezoned, ma'am? Why are you-"

"I will not tolerate this kind of-"

"Answer the question, Ms. Drake."

"I will not stand for this kind of interruption! You're a disgrace!"

"Answer the question, Councilwoman!"

Councilwoman Drake prepared to retort, but a gentle, large hand pushed the megaphone down. Bill Moss looked the councilwoman in the face, and said with sorrow and defeat, "Please, ma'am. Just answer the man's question."

Although the councilwoman continued to speak, her words were drowned out by the frustrated roar of the crowd. The neighbors screamed in disgust about betrayal and lies.

Mencken packed the blue megaphone in his backpack. With a grin of satisfaction at a job well done, he turned and left.

CHAPTER FIVE

Mencken pushed the steel grate door open. The store wasn't much – a ten-foot by five-foot space. The walls were covered with different types of booze. Nothing was refrigerated, and nothing was expensive. This was not where one went to buy fine wine. This was where one went to buy three dollar shot-sized bottles of Jack. The store didn't even have an official name. The red awning over the door simply read "Liquor."

Mencken went directly to the counter where a small Iranian man sat behind foot-and-a-half thick protective glass. A small, metal turnstile at counter level was the only means of passing things to the man at the register. The Iranian man was watching a soap-opera on a small, black tablet.

Mencken banged on the glass.

"Wait for commercial," the small man yelled, waving at Mencken without looking up from the program.

"Sahib," Mencken yelled. "You better turn that damn thing off, or I'll come over this counter."

Sahib waved again. "Shut up. Shut up. Greg is about to propose."

Mencken pushed the turnstile sideways and lean down

to look into the open space. "You better look up at me, or I'm going to propose an ass whooping."

Sahib waved a third time.

"SAHIB!" Mencken screamed.

The man threw his arms up in the air and turned, "What? What? What do you want? What can't wait a few more minutes? All I need is a few more minutes."

"I don't have time for your soaps, Sahib."

"Please," the man said, putting the turn style back to its original position. "You don't even have a real job. You have nothing but time." He took a pack of cigarettes off the rack behind him, opened the heavy door, stepped out of his protective box, retrieved a large key chain from his pocket, and locked the door behind him. "Whatever you want can happen outside. I'm on break."

"Inside. Outside. I don't care." Mencken followed the man out the front door.

On the sidewalk, in the bright sun, the man lit a cigarette and took a long drag.

"You going to offer me one?" Mencken asked even though he didn't smoke.

"Go buy your own," the man snapped. "Do I look like I have cigarettes lying around to spare? What do you want? Why are you here?"

"I want to know about what went down yesterday."

Sahib took another long drag. He was heavy and balding. Chest hair peeked out from the top of his shirt, partially covering the gold chain he wore. "Nothing happened. I opened the shop. I sold booze. I closed the shop. End of the story."

"Now you know," Mencken said with irritation, "that I'm not talking about here. With your wife. At the park."

"I don't know what you're talking about," Sahib said.

"Bullshit," Mencken exclaimed. "Your brother already sold you out. He told me your wife was there."

"He is an asshole. He doesn't know."

"Why are you holding out on me? You want me to

track down Maarit. You want me to bang on your front door. Wake up the baby. Is that what you want? Because I'll do it. I'll go right to your house. I know where you live."

Sahib laughed. "You go do that. That woman hasn't told me anything in ten years. If you get two words out of her, I'll give you my car. Then you could drive around town like a real man, instead of on that child's bicycle," Sahib motioned toward Mencken's motorcycle with his cigarette.

"Don't make fun of my baby."

"That is the ugliest baby I've ever seen. When are you going to find a woman and get a real car? Something that will hold car seats. Like a man."

"I don't need to explain myself to you."

Sahib pretended to cover his mouth in shock, "You're not gay, are you? Not that I care. Park your small, little baby in whatever garage you want. It's none of my business."

"I didn't want to have to do this, but you are forcing me. You are forcing me to do this."

"You've got nothing."

"Last month I happen to overhear a conversation. While I was at your community center. Covering that one big feast for you – remember? I got your center on the radio."

Sahib took another drag, refusing to acknowledge the event.

"That night, I was in the bathroom. Third stall. And you and your brother came in. And I happen to hear you and your brother talking about your father-in-law's visa. Something about not wanting to sponsor him to move to the States. Something about not wanting that 'arrogant asshole' around. Ring any bells?"

"You wouldn't," Sahib said, his eyes wide with fear.

"I mean, it's no Sam Dandrip radio piece, but I'll throw it up on my blog. Maybe with the title of 'Immigrants

Keep Immigrants Out?' Something like that?"

"Fine, asshole. What do you want to know?"

"I want to know what Maarit saw at the park yesterday."

"Stories. She always has wild stories. It's all lies. She's bored."

"Why don't you let me decide what's true and what's not. Just tell me what she saw."

"Okay, okay. She was at the park, taking a walk with the baby, and there was a new kid there."

"Dealing?" Mencken retrieved his notebook from his backpack and started taking notes.

"Of course he was dealing. That's all they do there."

"And she didn't know him?"

"No. He's new. Some new gang in the neighborhood. That's what I heard anyway. I don't care. I don't bother with their nonsense."

"Did he have a crew with him?"

"Sure, sure. They're never alone. She said there were three total."

"So what happened?"

"So this car pulls up, and this boy jumps out."

"What kind of car?"

"Oh sure, Maarit knows cars."

"So a boy jumps out?"

"Yeah. A boy jumps out, and runs up to the one with the stuff."

"How old is the boy?"

"She said he was like a short teenager."

"What'd he look like?"

"How would I know that? Was I there? Do you want the story or not?"

"I'm sorry. Keep going."

"Stop interrupting."

"I said I was sorry."

"You threaten me, and then interrupt me."

"I'm sorry. I said I was sorry."

"Okay, okay. Fine. So the teenager, he walks up to the dealer and punches him right in the balls. And then the other two, they come chasing after him. So he leads them back to the car. But a man steps out of the front seat and stabs both of the thugs with a knife. Super-fast. Maarit said she almost missed it, it was so quick. And both thugs went down. Then the man with the knife walked over to the dealer, who was still on the ground, and said something to him. Then the man and the teen got in the car and left."

"Did Maarit hear what he said?"

"No. She left. She didn't want to be there when the cops came. She just wants to walk in the park. I tell her not to get involved in their nonsense. Just walk, and then come home. So that is what she did."

"Do you know anything else about the two in the car?"

"No. She said it all happened fast. She didn't really see much. And like I said, she walked away. You know what happened to the two who were stabbed?"

Mencken was making notes. He didn't look up. "They weren't stabbed. Their throats were cut. They both bled out before the ambulance arrived. Died where there fell."

"Wow. No kidding," Sahib took another drag of his cigarette. "This city. We're moving soon. I'm going to sell this dump. We're going to the county."

"It's all there too, just more spread out."

"Eh, feels different."

Mencken finished making notes and returned his notebook to his backpack. "Thank you, Sahib. I appreciate you sharing that with me. I'll leave you out of whatever I write."

"We don't want any trouble."

"Don't worry. I won't even say I have a source."

"Do you know what it was all about?"

"I think there was a crew moving in on Agamemnon's turf without permission. It was a message."

"Usually, they just spray each other with bullets."

"Yeah," Mencken said, checking his phone. "There's a

new player in town. He's more elegant. He only works for the big players."

Sahib laughed and put his cigarette out on the sidewalk. "We are having a feast at the community center next month. You should come and cover it. Let the city know we aren't all terrorists. They seem to need reminding all the time. "

Mencken shook Sahib's hand. "I'll be there. Shoot me an email and let me know when."

"Thank you, friend," Sahib said, and the two men parted ways.

CHAPTER SIX

The basement of Saint Jude Thaddeus Catholic Church was a large square room with a gray concrete floor and white, rectangular ceiling tiles. The florescent lights buzzed. The room was full of round tables, which were filled with anxious neighbors. The air was muggy and thick with anxiety.

Mencken sat in the back, between two, large, elderly women. Both fanned themselves with the flyers they'd been given at the door. Both wore formless dresses. He looked over at the coffee station Father McFadden had set up. Stacks of white Styrofoam cups, sugar packets, and a can of powdered creamer stood between two large silver coffee urns.

"Would you lovely ladies like some coffee," Mencken said, standing.

The one on the right said, "Sitting next to a fine man like you is probably all the excitement I can take tonight, baby."

"You know that's right," the one on the left said.

Mencken laughed. "Okay then," he said. "I'll be right back." On his way to the coffee, he surveyed the room. Two men stood out among the Cherry Hill residents. The first was the mayor's tax assessor; a mousy man dressed in a rumpled suit, and, including Father McFadden, the other Caucasian in the room. The second man of note was Nathaniel Davis, the city council representative from District Ten. He was a thin, thirty-something, ladder-climber who had moved into the district in order to run for the city council seat. His gray suit was clearly tailored for his jogger's frame. The outfit was completed by shiny black shoes and a red bowtie. His mayoral ambitions were not a secret.

When Father McFadden took the podium, Mencken took his seat. The kind priest raised his hand and the room grew silent. "Thank you," he said, "for coming tonight. I didn't expect such a great turnout. I appreciate you all giving up your Wednesday night to be here. To start off the night, I've invited Reverend Jeremiah Leaks to open us in prayer."

The room muttered affirmation as a heavyset, African American man in a black suit and tie, took the stage. "Let us pray," he boomed. His voice was deep, rich, and full of authority.

Mencken watched as everyone in the room bowed their heads and closed their eyes. Several people raised hands in the air. There was a stabbing pain on Mencken's left foot. He winced and looked down. The elderly woman's brown cane was grinding into his toe. He looked up at her with a mix of rage and confusion. She mouthed, "Bow your head and close your eyes, baby." Mencken smiled and complied.

Reverend Leaks prayed, "I will lift up mine eyes unto the hills, from whence cometh my help. My help cometh from the Lord, which made heaven and earth."

Confirmation echoed through the room.

Reverend Leaks began to pick up the intensity. "He will not suffer thy foot to be moved: he that keepeth thee will not slumber."

Murmured agreements followed.

"He will not suffer thy foot to be moved," Reverend

Leaks boomed.

"Amen," people said.

"He will not suffer thy foot to be moved," Reverend Leaks repeated.

"That's right. Amen. That's right," the room responded.

"He. Will. Not. Suffer. Thy. Foot. To. Be. Moved." Each word pounded the air, seemingly shaking the room.

People began to clap.

"The Lord shall preserve thee from all evil. He. Shall. Preserve. Thy. Soul."

The room responded again with loud and vibrant approval.

"The Lord," Reverend said, reaching his climax. "The Lord," he repeated again, with more power. "The Lord shall preserve thy going out and thy coming in. From this time forth. And even. And even. Forevermore."

People stood and yelled with joy, shouting their approval.

"As it is written," Reverend Leaks declared. "Let it be done, Lord Jesus."

Almost the entire room was on their feet, yelling their agreement with hands held high.

Reverend Leaks took his seat at the front table. Father McFadden returned to the podium. "Thank you, Reverend, for those powerful words. Now, we must get to the reason we have gathered here today. The Mayor has sent to us Mister Leonard Silverstein to explain to us the coming changes in our neighborhood. I'll now give the podium to Mister Silverstein from the Office of Tax Assessment."

"The Office of Tax Assessment? Well, this should be riveting," the grandmother sitting to Mencken's right said. Mencken and the other elderly woman laughed.

Silverstein fumbled with his notes at the podium. The silence of the room was thick. The rustling of his paper stabbed at it, bringing pain to everyone's ears. "Yes," he said, adjusting his glasses. "Well. Thank you for having me tonight."

The room was stoic.

A bead of sweat ran down his balding head. He wiped it away from his forehead with the sleeve of his suit. "I, well. I appreciate you having me here. As I'm sure you know," he continued, looking at his notes. "The mayor's office has approved the waterfront property along Waterfront Avenue for development. This includes, but is not limited to, large portions of Middle Branch Park."

"What are we supposed to do without our park?" a young father in the back yelled. "Where do you expect our kids to play if you take away their fields?"

Mumbles of angry support resonated in the room.

"I'm sorry, sir," Silverstein replied. "I'm not here to debate the merits of the decision. I'm here to discuss the change in zoning's potential impact on you. As you have probably heard, the property has already been purchased by Building Baltimore. They have contracted with the city to construct luxury waterfront homes on the land."

"This is some bullshit," another man yelled. The room agreed with intense frustration.

"Well, I understand that." Silverstein began to fumble with his notes.

Councilman Davis came to his rescue. Swooping up to the podium with hands raised in a gesture of peace, Davis said, "Calm down everyone. Calm down. Now I know that change is difficult. I know it's hard. But this is good for us. This is good for our district. Let's hear Mister Silverstein out."

"Thank you, Councilman," Silverstein continued. "Well, as I was saying, according to Baltimore tax code, your property taxes for the following year will be based not on the estimate of your house, but rather on the estimate of the property in your community. This means that when the property value of a neighborhood increases, well, so does the annual property taxes."

"Don't matter," a young woman in the back yelled. "I don't pay property taxes anyhow." The room laughed.

"This is a misnomer, ma'am. This change may affect you as well," Silverstein continued. "For example, if you live in Section Eight housing, you might be relocated."

"Relocated," an elderly man at a middle table exclaimed.

"This is bullshit," another man yelled.

The room erupted with frustration.

"Well, again," Silverstein said. "We aren't here today to argue whether or not these things should be passed. They have been passed already. We are here to discuss how you can best prepare yourself."

The volume of anger in the room grew, forcing Silverstein to stop and wait. Speaking louder, he continued, "If you do own your home, well, after the construction of the luxury homes, your property taxes will increase twenty percent a year until they have stabilized with the value of the property in the area. If you are in government subsidized housing, you will be given three years before mandatory relocation."

"This is my home," an elderly woman cried. "I'm not leaving my home. Where do you think I can go? This is my home."

The room broke into chaotic agreement, everyone voicing their frustrations at once.

Again Davis sought to come to the rescue. He stepped back in, again with his hands raised. "People, people," he yelled. "Quiet down. Get control of yourselves. Yelling at Mister Silverstein won't do any good."

Mencken spotted his opportunity. Standing, and then stepping up on his chair so that he towered over the room, he called out, "Councilman Davis. Excuse me. I have a question."

The brazen command in his voice drew the attention of the room.

"And you are?" the councilman replied.

"Mencken Cassie. Representing the Baltimore Star." With all eyes on him, Mencken stepped down from the chair. "Tomorrow we will be running an article on these proceedings. Would you be able to confirm for us tonight that you received sixty-five thousand dollars in campaign donations from the Ignite Baltimore Fund?"

"I'm sorry, Mister Cassie did you say? This isn't the time or place for that discussion."

"Could you also confirm for us that the Ignite Baltimore Fund is a subsidiary of The Building Baltimore? Is it true, Councilman that you received a large donation last year from the very development company that is now destroying a beloved park in your district and economically pressuring residents to leave their homes?"

Davis attempted to respond, but he could not be heard over the fury in the room. Residents yelled and banged on the table. Some stormed out. Others screamed their disapproval at the podium.

Davis screamed loudly, "You have no proof. You have no proof."

Mencken silently sat back down and watch the room continue to erupt.

The grandmother to his right leaned into his ear and whispered, "Baby, you just made a big mess."

Mencken smiled and sipped his coffee.

CHAPTER SEVEN

Mencken entered Imani's with pride in his eyes and five copies of the Baltimore Star under his arm. The place was quiet. It was too early for the breakfast rush, much earlier than Mencken usually arrived. Only a few of the tables were filled.

An infamous homeless man named Spencer sat in the corner to the left of the door. He was eating a bagel and sipping a coffee from a white Styrofoam cup. Spencer was a celebrity on the neighborhood Facebook page. He was known for peeing where he shouldn't, picking flowers he thought were pretty from people's planters, and occasionally shattering car windows to grab change left in the front console. Mencken nodded to him. Spencer smiled and pointed back.

Mencken made it a point to keep a working relationship with two or three homeless people in every neighborhood. They were the invisible eyes and ears of the city. They saw everything, but no one saw them.

A few tables over from Spencer were two people Mencken didn't recognize: a young woman in a charcoal business suit and a man in jeans and a t-shirt. Their feet touched under the table. Both had large breakfast platters in front of them. Mencken noticed the large, sparkling, diamond ring on the woman's finger. The man had a laptop bag hung over the back of his chair. Mencken thought they looked cute together.

Abby Deces was working the griddle behind the bar. Three pounds of bacon slowly sizzled in front of her. Abby was tall and thin, with flowing blond hair and bright blue eyes. She had the looks of an A-list Hollywood actress. Currently, she was pursuing a degree in political science at Hopkins, but Mencken couldn't remember if she was in her junior or senior year. Abby worked mornings at Imani's. She opened the place up on weekdays and left around eleven to catch her first class.

Mencken crossed the room to her. "Hey Abby," he said with a grin. "Check this out." He passed her one of the newspapers from under his arm.

Abby flipped the bacon with a giant silver spatula, and then turned and took the paper from him. She unfolded the bundle and scanned it. "Is there something specific I should be looking for?" she asked. Her green apron was tied tightly, exaggerating her breasts.

"Read the headline," he said.

"Okay," she said.

"No, no. Read it out loud."

She sighed. "Fine. 'Corrupt Councilman.' I read it this morning. Nathaniel Davis was caught with his pants down at a town hall meeting. Probably the end of his career. What of it?"

"Read the byline."

"Hey, check that out. 'By Mencken Cassie.' You made the front page of the Star. Congratulations. That's great."

But Mencken wasn't sure it was great. On one hand, the reporter in him was excited to make the front page. It was every reporters' dream to see their name above the fold. On the other hand, hearing the words come from another person's mouth made him feel like a sellout. In theory, Mencken loved being independent. He shouldn't care if the establishment approved of him. The indie side of him wished he could shrug it off. "Front page? Whatever. It's about time they printed something worth the ink." But the other half of him was a giddy school girl. "Looky, looky! The front page! The front page!"

"Thanks," he said in reply, trying to hide the confusion in his heart.

"Really, congratulations," she said, handing the paper back.

A new wave of confused emotions filled Mencken. He didn't know what he expected her to do with it. Maybe hang it on the wall? Maybe ask him to sign it? Handing it back was not an option in his mind. Disgruntled at the lack of accolade he'd received, he stomped off to his normal table in the back, across from the door.

He pulled from his backpack his laptop and cracked it open. An email from his mom was waiting for him. The subject line was, "My baby made the front page!" His heart warmed. That was what he needed.

Abby brought coffee in a large, white mug. She gently placed it on the table in front of him. "Now that you're famous, you'll have to pay for the coffee," she said. "And I expect a tip."

Mencken watched her walk away, unsure if she was teasing. He checked the stats of his blog. There'd already been a slight bump this morning. He assumed it was the Star's online copy. It had a link to his site at the bottom.

Imani descended the steps that led from behind the bar to her apartment upstairs. She was comfortably dressed in dark gray sweats and a black t-shirt. Mencken sipped his coffee, trying to decide if she'd recently cut her hair again. Thinking of her keeping it short so she wouldn't have to mess with it made him smile. She joined Abby at the griddle and started putting plates together. Mencken hoped one was for him.

Another email came through. It was from Winchell. He wanted a follow-up for tomorrow's page two – interviews with neighbors and a response from City Hall. Mencken had already written it. He'd gotten the quotes from the neighbors last night, immediately following the meeting. He'd called contacts in the mayor's office after he'd gotten home. They, of course, denied any knowledge of financial contributions to Councilman Davis and completely rejected the assertion that he'd had anything to do with the decision to rezone the park. Before going to bed, Mencken hammered out a tight seven-hundred words, combining all the quotes into one piece. He didn't tell Winchell that though. He simply said, "I'll get right on it." No need for Winchell to get an inside peek at how Mencken spent his days.

Imani carried a tray with three steaming plates and two cups of coffee toward Mencken. She pulled up a table before him and laid the plates out. Each one contained pancakes, eggs, bacon, a slab of fried ham, and a few orange slices. Mencken reached over to snag a piece of bacon. He was shocked when Imani swatted his hand away.

"This ain't for you. You want food, go tell Abby," Imani chided.

"You going to eat all of those by yourself?" Mencken said, sitting back in his chair.

"No, it's for me and my boys," Imani said as she laid out three sets of silverware.

"I thought I was your boy," he said with a curious grin. He didn't know Imani had any "boys."

"Awe, that's sweet," she teased. "You think just because you're a front page journalist now, that you're going to get special treatment. Sorry, Hon. You still have to order like everyone else."

Mencken was surprised when the floor to his left rumbled. A hatch in the floor came open and a young teen emerged from it. He was short and thin, with a shaved head and an optimistic smile. He wore jeans that were a little too big for him and a white t-shirt. He bounded passed Mencken, pulled out a chair at Imani's table, sat down, and began eating.

"Who's this?" Mencken asked.

"Mencken, meet Jose. Jose, Mencken," Imani said, pulling out a chair for herself and spreading a cloth napkin in her lap.

Jose turned to face Mencken. With a piece of bacon in his right hand, he reached out with his left and touched Mencken's arm. "Huh?" he said. Then he turned back to his own plate.

"What'd you think?" Imani said.

"He's undecided," Jose said as he shoveled scrambled eggs into his mouth. Mencken was amazed that a kid so small could eat so much.

"What do you mean I'm undecided?" Mencken said, leaning forward.

"Just that," Jose said, looking back with a smile. "You're undecided." Jose reached for a cup of coffee, but Imani swatted his hand. He recoiled, holding his hand like a wounded puppy guarding a hurt paw. "Come on. I need a pick-me-up."

"You're too young," Imani said, sipping from her mug. "It'll stunt your growth."

"So Jose is your - your son?" Mencken asked, confused. Besides their short haircuts, there was no perceivable similarity between them.

"No," Jose said. "I'm her boy." Then he held his fist out of a fist bump from Imani.

"You know it," she replied, returning the gesture.

"I'm sorry. Your boy?" Mencken said, but before anyone could explain, another figure emerged from the basement. "I didn't even know you had a basement," Mencken said. "You keeping a small village down there or something?"

"Just my boys," Imani said.

"Because I'm her boy," Jose said again, offering another fist bump, which Imani returned again.

"How have I never met your boys before?" Mencken said, his bewilderment building.

"Because you're never here before ten," Imani replied.

"Imani's boys go to work early," Jose said, his mouth full of ham. "And I'm her boy." A third fist bump followed.

The man who emerged from the basement was quite different from Jose. He was tanned with sandy brown hair. He wore a light blue polo shirt that was tucked tightly into blue jeans. He was lean and just under six-foot. His build reminded Mencken of a featherweight professional fighter. He walked with precision, like a man who had somewhere important to be.

"Mencken, Chris. Chris, Mencken," Jose said.

Chris nodded to Mencken and took the seat next to Imani. Placing his hand gently on her arm, he said softly, "Thank you. You don't have to do this every morning."

Imani smiled. She gazed into his eyes and replied, "I want to do this. Every morning. This is important to me."

"You're going to spoil us," Chris replied.

"Good," she said, touching his arm with her free hand.

"The pancakes are great," Jose exclaimed, as he took a sip of Imani's coffee while her hands were occupied.

An overwhelming range of emotions tore through Mencken as he watched the scene unfold. He was angry at his ignorance. These two had been living below his table this entire time and he had no idea? How had he missed that? And who was this man? What right did he have to touch Imani's arm? These two clearly weren't related. They looked nothing alike. Mencken couldn't take it anymore. He had to know. He closed his laptop, picked up his chair, and moved it to their table, forcing himself between Imani and Jose.

"What's the word on this one?" Chris said, taking a bit of bacon and giving a slight nod in Mencken's direction.

"Undecided," Jose said, not looking up from his almost finished pancakes.

"What does that mean?" Mencken said, frustrated.

"Undecided means no decision has been made," Chris said factually.

Imani laughed. "Thought you'd know that one, being a writer and all," she added with a belittling, mothering tone.

"But you know what they say," Chris said pointing his fork at Jose. "Never trust a man with a last name for a first name."

"Who says that?" Mencken said.

"It's a thing," Jose replied.

"It's not a thing," Mencken said. "No one says that."

"As if we'd trust your opinion on it. That's just what a man with a last name for a first name would say," Chris said with a smile.

"Right?" Jose said.

"Are you serious with these two?" Mencken said, pleading for Imani to make some sense out of all of this.

"I'm her boy," Jose said. A fourth fist bump was delivered.

"Probably because you have a proper first name," Chris said.

"So you live in the basement?" Mencken said, trying to change the subject.

"I wouldn't say that," Chris said.

"What would you say?" Mencken retorted.

"About what?" Chris asked.

"About living here," Mencken shot back.

"We do sleep here," Jose offered.

"And eat here," Imani said.

"And sometimes we use your shower upstairs," Jose said.

"But do you live here?" Imani replied.

"I don't know. A lot of people eat here," Jose said.

"And if you fell asleep at a table, I wouldn't kick you out," Imani said. "Under those conditions, Mencken lives here too," Imani said.

Jose leaned in close to Mencken to tell him a secret.

"Abby would though. She's not undecided in any way. Rotten to the core."

"Hard working and focused," Imani corrected. "We call her hardworking and focused."

"I could never live with someone I couldn't trust," Chris said.

"Maybe we could change his name," Jose said to Chris. "How do you feel about Bruce?" he asked Mencken.

"So how long have you lived here?" Mencken interjected, trying to bring a mature tone back to the conversation.

"We don't, Bruce," Chris said.

"You sleep here. You eat here. You live here," Mencken said.

"Spencer sleeps and eats here too," Imani said. She waved to the homeless man across the room who had heard his name. He smiled and pointed at her.

"How long have you been sleeping in the basement?" Mencken asked.

"About eleven months," Jose answered.

"Eleven hours," Chris corrected. "Eleven months, that's absurd. No one sleeps that long."

"Rip Van Winkle slept that long," Imani said.

"True," Jose replied.

"But he lived in a different time," Chris argued. "We're busier now."

"Are we?" Imani said. "I mean, farming's a lot of work."

"How would you know?" Jose said.

"I have storehouses of knowledge you know nothing of," Imani said.

"It's true," Chris added. "I've seen them. Tall ceilings."

"What do you do for a living?" Mencken asked Chris.

"I'm a superhero," Jose answered. Chris laughed.

"Oh really?" Mencken said.

"Yep," Jose said with a smile. "I fight monsters."

"What about you?" Mencken asked Chris.

"I'm no hero," Chris replied sincerely.

"So what do you do?" Mencken clarified.

"When?" Chris said.

"What do you mean when?" Mencken asked, growing frustrated with this game.

"I'm just trying to answer your question," Chris said, sipping his coffee. "When do you want to know what I do?"

"It was your question, Bruce. Don't get snippy," Jose said. Then turning to Chris he added, "I think he wants to know right now."

"Oh," Chris said. "Right now I'm eating breakfast."

"No, no," Jose said. "He wants you to answer the question right now."

"Well, I just did," Chris replied. He then turned to Imani and said, "You said he was a reporter?"

"He's a little slow this morning," Imani said, patting Mencken's arm.

Mencken turned his attention back to the boy. "How old are you?" he asked.

"Thirteen," Jose replied. "But I'm very mature for my age."

"Where do you go to school?" Mencken asked.

Jose dramatically looked off into the distance. "The world is my school," he said. "Every street and alley holds new lessons."

"He's home-schooled," Chris said.

"By you?" Mencken asked.

"Oh no," Chris said. "He's already passed what I can teach him. Besides, he doesn't listen to me." Chris gave a knowing wink to Jose.

"I've got skills," Jose said with pride.

"I'm teaching him math and English," Imani said. "Abby is managing his history and social studies curriculum. He's actually very bright, even if he's not showing it now," she said, pushing Jose's head.

"Abby's mean," Jose whispered again with a smile.

"Watch out."

Mencken's phone began to buzz in his pocket. He took it out and looked at the screen. It was a call he needed to take, or at least call back soon. Looking at Chris, he smiled and said, "So let me get this straight. You're superheroes who live in the basement of Imani's restaurant. He's homeschooled, and you're a smartass that doesn't answer direct questions."

"You're catching on, Bruce," Chris said with a smile. Imani laughed.

Jose looked up from his plate and said to Imani, "I like this one. We should keep him."

Mencken's phone rang again. He glanced down, it was the same number. He knew he couldn't miss the opportunity it offered. Standing, he asked, "What did you say your last name was?" he asked Chris.

"I didn't," Chris replied, focusing again on his breakfast. "Please pass the salt and pepper," he said to Jose. The boy obliged.

"Alright then," Mencken said. "It was fascinating talking to you, Chris with no last name."

"Same, Bruce Mencken," Chris said.

"We'll pick this up later," Mencken promised as he gathered his things. He thanked Imani for the coffee and walked toward the door. His phone rang again as he stepped onto the sidewalk.

"You've got Mencken," he said into the phone.

"Councilman Black will see you if you can arrive at his office within the next fifteen minutes," a proper-sounding voice said on the other end.

"Be right there," Mencken replied.

CHAPTER EIGHT

"I didn't rush over here to sit around and wait," Mencken barked at the small aide who had come to check on him. Mencken had arrived at the historic rowhome on Saint Paul within four minutes, well within the fifteen-minute timeline he'd been given on the phone. Upon arrival, he had been escorted into a small, luxurious living room, and then left to wait for over an hour.

"I assure you, Mr. Cassie, meeting with you is at the top of the Councilman's priorities, but the demands of his job do not slow because you have arrived."

It hadn't taken Mencken long to start hating the aide and his proper ways. The man was at least a foot-and-a-half shorter than Mencken. His white three-piece suit was contrasted by his thick black-rimmed glasses. "I can't sit here all day," Mencken said, pacing behind one of the leather couches.

"I haven't seen you sit yet, Mr. Cassie," the aide said with a deadpan stare. "Are you sure I can't get you something to drink? Coffee? Tea? A soda?"

"No. I just want to speak with the councilman. You asked me to come here. And now I'm here. Why did you have me rush over here just to wait in this damn room?

I've got other appointments I need to keep today with people even more important than Councilman Black." Of course Mencken was lying. Besides a few leads he intended to chase, his schedule was completely clear.

"I'm sure you have many important meetings, Mr. Cassie. I'm sure you do," the aide said as he backed out of the room, closing the two heavy, sliding, mahogany doors behind him.

At least they'd put Mencken in a nice room. Mencken had heard stories of people being left on the front porch or in the entryway as they waited to meet with Councilman Black. In the center of the space was a leather couch opposed by two, matching, leather chairs. Between them was a dark coffee table with ornately carved legs. On the wall opposite the door was a large, white marble, fireplace. The mantle was littered with pictures of the councilman with his arm around various celebrities. On either side of the fire place were bookcases full of old volumes of law books.

Councilman Black had ruled the Baltimore city council for almost two decades. He'd been a career politician for over forty years. Publically, his ambition had never spread past the council president seat. Every time a state or national legislative seat came open, his name was tossed around by the media, but Black had never shown the smallest interest.

Mencken was jarred from his thoughts when the large doors moved again. After pushing both doors fully open, the aide stood at attention to the left of the doorway.

Councilman Black strolled through the newly open space. Standing six-foot and weighing in at three-hundred-twenty pounds, Councilman Black was a boulder of a man. As always, he was dressed in a black, three-piece, tailored suit. His vest was gray and white checkered. Although his breathing was heavy, he was surprisingly spry for such a large man.

The councilman's eyes darted up and down Mencken,

sizing him up. Approaching quickly with an outstretched hand, Black said, "Mr. Cassie. Thank you. For coming." The councilman's voice was deep and stuffed with cotton. His soft, moisture filled breathing forced him to pause between each word. The deep resonance mixed with his small wheeze made every word sound like a chore. "I appreciate. You coming. To my private office. City Hall is. So busy. No space. To converse."

"Thank you for seeing me, Councilman," Mencken said, shaking the large man's hand.

The councilman strolled over to a small cart next to the fireplace that held glass jars full of various liquors and heavy tumblers. He turned a tumbler over and filled it with thick, amber liquid. "Would you. Like some?" he said holding up the glass. The pauses within his sentence were so large, it was difficult to tell whether he had finished speaking or not.

"No. Thank you," Mencken replied. "It's a little early in the morning for me."

"It's only early. If you sleep," the councilman said, with a smile. "Please. Sit," he said, motioning to the couch.

Mencken took a seat. The councilman sat across from him in one of the straight-back chairs. He withdrew a thick cigar from his coat pocket. The aide rushed over, clipped the end of the stick, and then lit it while the councilman took a drag. The tip glowed red and smoke seeped out from the sides of the councilman's mouth. Once the cigar was lit, the aide returned to his post.

Holding his smoking cigar in one hand and his whiskey in the other, the councilman said, "Your mother. Attends New Eden Baptist Church."

"She does," Mencken replied, his defenses rising at the odd statement. "Is that why you called me here? To talk about my mother's church?"

"I also attend. New Eden. In fact. I am a deacon."

"Okay?"

"Maybe she and I. Have run into. Each other."

Mencken reached into his backpack, which was sitting on the floor next to the couch, and retrieved his notepad. He took the pen from behind his ear and prepared to take notes. "I appreciate you allowing me to interview you, sir. I have several questions about -"

"I'm sorry," the councilman interrupted. "For the confusion. This is not. An interview. I just. Wanted to get to know you."

"Oh," Mencken said, trying to hide his disappointment. He'd had a standing request with the councilman's office for an interview going on two years. "I'd much rather talk about you, sir. For example, I'd love to talk about some of the projects happening in your district."

"Lighten up, Mr. Cassie. There'll be. Plenty of time. For those things. Tell me. About yourself. Graduated from City High School. Yes?"

"That's right," Mencken said.

"Then. You went to. UMBC. Where you. Majored in English."

"It seems you already know everything about me," Mencken said, leaning back.

"Tell me. Why not. Take a job. At an established paper? I'm sure. At this point. There have been. Offers."

"I'm not much of a team player," Mencken said with a grin. "You, on the other hand, played football for Maryland? Middle line-backer, right?"

The councilman smiled and took another pull on his cigar. "I would think. An ambitious man. Like yourself. Would leap at the. Prestige of. The Washington Post."

Mencken smiled.

"I know. They've made inquiries."

"I like it here. This city needs me."

He took another drag and blew the smoke at the ceiling. "What do you. Hope. Will be. Your legacy?"

"I'd ask the same of you," Mencken retorted.

"I'm not like you. Mr. Cassie. I'm just. A humble. Civil servant. I'm not. Shooting for the stars."

"I'm devoting my life to bringing the dark places of Baltimore into the light," Mencken said with pride. "This city needs a little truth."

"You are. An interesting man. I'd hoped. We could. Be friends."

"Now that's interesting. What, exactly, is the cost of your friendship?"

"Respect. Sir. My friends. Respect. One another."

"Do you perceive that I don't respect you?"

"You. Don't respect. My friends," the councilman said, smoking his cigar again.

"I'm not sure what you mean," Mencken said with a factious grin.

"Last night. Councilman Davis. That was. Disrespectful."

"Listen," Mencken said, growing frustrated.

"And ambushing. Councilwoman. Drake. At a simple rally. Again. That was. Disrespectful."

"I'm just doing my job, sir."

"There is. A fine line. Between passionate ambition. And ignorant. Reckless flailing.

Mencken's blood bubbled with rage. "I'm not interested in being lectured by you. I tell the truth. That's my job. My job is to tell the people the truth."

"It used to be. That the press. And City Hall. Respected. One another."

"I'm no one's puppet."

"I don't disagree. That telling the truth. Is your job. But last night? Or at the rally? That. Was not. About truth. It was. A spectacle. A side show. Last night. Was about you."

Mencken crossed his arms. "Why don't we change subjects? Tell me about the city council's plans for Old Towne Mall. I've heard it's going to be sold next year?"

"Why. Are you. So uncomfortable. Talking. About you? Let's stay. Focused on. On the. Circus. You seem. To want to. Be the ringmaster of."

"That's nonsense. I'm not the one selling out the

people of their neighborhood. I'm not the one saying one thing and doing another."

"Some of my friends. Are at Hopkins. Your mother. She likes her job. As a nurse. Over twenty years. It would be. A shame if."

"You leave my mom alone," Mencken growled with rage.

"And you. Spend time. At a bar. The owner is. Imani Douglas. You seem. To be fond of her."

"So you know a few things about me, I won't-"

"Her liquor license. Is set. To be renewed. It would. Be a shame. If she. Were to lose. It. After so long in-"

His fist and teeth clenched tight, Mencken struggled to keep control of his anger. He knew this was a game. He knew he needed to remain unmoved, but knowing and doing were two very different things. "I'm not afraid of you," he sneered. "And I won't be intimidated. You don't scare me."

Black smiled. "Please. We are just. Getting to know. One another. Are you sure. You don't. Want. A drink?"

"Is there anything of substance you want to discuss? Or am I only here to watch you flex your muscles."

The councilman took a long drag on his cigar. "I understand. That you are young. And your blood. Runs hot. For glory. And Fame. I'd like to ask. That in the future. When you have a story. You show us. Your elders. The elders of the city. You claim. To love. Some respect. And give us warning. Before you surprise us. At a town hall meeting. Or rally. In our own backyard."

"Decades of corruption and poor leadership have earned you nothing with me."

"You. Have a bright. Future. I can help. I'm a good friend."

"You've got me all wrong. I don't care about fame or glory. All I care about is my city and the truth."

"Your city?"

"Yeah. My city."

"I think. You and I. Are not. So different." Councilman Black took another long drag. The smoke hung in the ceiling of the room like a cloud on a windless day. "But you. See truth. Every time. You look in the mirror. Whereas. I see. Possibility. Let's talk more. About. Your story."

Black glanced at the doors and the aide again snapped into action. Stepping into the hallway, he grabbed a manila envelope and rushed it to the Councilman's side.

The councilman leaned forward and placed his cigar and drink on the coffee table. He then received the envelope and looked inside. "You see. I understand. Your story." He pulled two photos from the envelope and laid them on the coffee table.

"How did you get those?" Mencken said with shock. The photos were of the walls in his apartment: one of his map and one of his tree of corruption. Mencken felt violated and angry. Looking closely, he could tell they were recent because his notes from last night were on the wall. "This is completely against the law. You broke into my house. Is that why you had me wait so long? So one of your thugs could go rummage through my apartment? This is kindergarten crap. I expected more from you."

"No. No. You are. Confused," the councilman said with a smile. "No one. Broke in. This morning. You see. You were there." The councilman dropped a third photo on the table. It was of Mencken, curled up, in his bed, fast asleep.

Mencken swallowed, taking in the implications of the final photo.

"Now. Mr. Cassie. I know. You believe. You've uncovered. Something. With this. Cabal fantasy. And. Good for you. I wish you. The best. With all that. It will make. An interesting story. All I ask. Is that you. Show my colleagues. And I. Some respect. And we. Will do likewise."

A fire burned in Mencken's stomach, rage mixed with

fear and confusion. The emotions made him dizzy. He couldn't pull his eyes from the photo. The photographer couldn't have been less than three feet away from him. "I don't respond well to threats," he said, softly.

When the councilman laughed, his entire body jiggled. "No one. Is threatening. Anyone. Mr. Cassie. We are just. Sharks. Circling one another. In the same bowl."

The councilman withdrew a fourth picture from his envelope and passed it to Mencken. It was a professional, head shot of the councilman. Mencken looked up with confusion.

"For the, um. Art project. On your wall. The other picture of me. Isn't flattering." The councilman reached forward, took up his cigar, stood, and began to leave the room. "Thank you, again. Mr. Cassie," he called without looking back. "It was good. To meet you. In person."

CHAPTER NINE

Menken was sure he was right. He'd studied his wall for hours last night, trying to predict the next move. All signs pointed here. "Well, not here, exactly," he explained. "But definitely to her."

Rosie sighed, pulled her hair back into a ponytail and secured it with a hair band. "I thought you were being ironic when you said you wanted me to join you on a stakeout. I thought we might get dinner or something. Maybe catch a movie. I should have known better."

They sat in Rosie's unmarked car and watched the front door of a warehouse from across the street. They didn't look at each other, rather they watched intently, waiting for signs of Mencken's prediction to come true.

"I mean, she's the key to the neighborhood's redevelopment," Mencken continued. "If you get rid of her, the school closes. And if you close the school, the last hope in the neighborhood is dead. And if the last hope is dead, the door is open for a savior. It all makes sense. It has to be her."

"And there's a new episode of the Walking Dead on tonight. You're making me miss the Walking Dead. Tomorrow everyone's going to tell me who died. It's not even worth watching the episode once you know who died."

"And it's got to be today. Today or tomorrow. In two days there's a film crew coming down from Boston to interview her for a documentary about fighting urban blight. And you know, if I could find out about the documentary, then they found out about it. They absolutely know about it. So, if they don't get her today or tomorrow, then, well, then it's too late. Then she's a martyr because her story is out there in posterity. Right now, she'll just be a do-gooder swallowed by the city."

"And you didn't even bring coffee. Don't you know that on a stakeout, especially at night, you always bring coffee? Always. Who sits in a car on a stakeout without coffee? Or snacks. You brought no snacks. You're making me sit in this car with no coffee and no snacks."

"I was going through her daily routine. This is the only time she is out of her own neighborhood. Every night she comes here for an hour. If it were me, this is where I'd do it. This has to be the spot."

"Do you know how much time I spend in this car? I'm in this car most of the damn day. I don't want to be in this car while I'm off duty. Damn it. I hate this damn car."

"They can't get her in her own neighborhood. The block wouldn't stand for it. She means too much. It has to be here. This is the spot."

"What'cha doing Rosie?" Rosie said, mocking Mencken's deep voice. "I'm going to sit in a car for hours and stare at a building. Want to come?" She pretended to giggle and then said in her most girly voice, "Oh sure, Mencken. I'd love to. That sounds amazing. Oh, what? You don't have a car? Sure. We can take mine."

"It'll be a mugging. At first, I thought maybe a drive-by. But this guy is all about the craft. He won't stoop to a drive-by. He'll use a knife. Or his hands. It's becoming his signature. You know, the street gangs have started calling him 'The Reaper.' Like he's some comic book character.

'The Reaper.' So stupid. He's just a killer. And they said he's recruiting a gang of kids. So far, I've only heard stories of one kid with him. But maybe's there's more? Maybe he brings different kids on different jobs. It feels like a whole, disgusting, child soldier thing, but I don't think they're drugged. I think it's more like a gathering of outcasts, like in Oliver Twist, but instead of stealing they're –"

"Who did you say this woman is again?" Rosie's voice had gone cold. There was an icy focus on her face.

"Anita? Anita Dickson. She runs a charter school near the Perkins projects on the east side."

"I know where Perkins is. Why do you think she's in trouble?"

"Her school is just south of Old Town Mall. There's a member of the Cabal making a move on Old Town Mall for redevelopment, but I think he's going to try and wrap the surrounding area into it. He needs to get rid of more residents first through before he can buy up all the blocks he'll need. Her school is the only thing keeping people there. It's a neighborhood-based elementary school, focused on kids from a limited geographic area." Mencken paused, realizing the atmosphere in the car had changed. "Wait. Why are you suddenly interested?"

"Because that car," Rosie said, pointing at a beat up El Camino parked a block away, "has circled the block four times, and now they've parked. There're two people in it. Just sitting there with their lights off."

"Oh shit," Mencken said with excitement. "I was right. I can't believe I was right."

"Calm down," Rosie said as she leaned over Mencken and opened the glove box. She took a small lockbox from the inside. Quickly, she turned the dials. "We don't know anything."

"I mean, I was just putting puzzle pieces together. You know? I can't believe I nailed it."

"Breathe, Slugger. Nothing's happened yet." Rosie got the box open and withdrew a SIG Sauer P398. She checked the ammo.

"Oh shit," Mencken exclaimed as she withdrew the weapon. "Is that a gun?"

"You know I'm a cop, right?" Rosie said, jamming the gun into the back of her jeans. "What's this place again?"

"It's a P90X workout center. Really, it's just a big warehouse. They just opened it, like, three months ago. They don't even have a sign yet."

A small door leading into the side of the warehouse opened. Out stepped two women, both in workout gear with towels around their necks. They were laughing.

"That's her," Mencken said, pointing. "That's Anita. She's the one on the left."

"Great," Rosie said, but her attention was focused on the car up the street. She tensed when the passenger side door swung open. Out stepped a small man, or maybe it was a child? He wore all black, including black gloves and a black ski mask.

"It's going down now," Rosie said. There was a new tone of command in her voice. She opened her car door and stepped into the street. Crouching down to the level of the car window, but not taking her eyes off the road, she said, "Stay in the car."

Mencken watched the boy in the ski mask as he moved, slowly toward the two women. The women sat and chatted by the door, clueless to the doom on their heels.

Rosie stood, motionless, in front of the car, waiting until the small figure in black was directly in front of her. Mencken saw the assailant pull a knife from his pants. It glimmered in the streetlight. Rosie must have seen it too because she held her out with both hands. "Police!" she yelled. "Stay where you are!"

The would-be mugger froze, staring at her. The women screamed at the sight of the assailant in black and the woman with the raised gun. Rosie yelled again, "Put the knife on the down! Lay down on the ground!"

Shots rang out. Three in succession. The pops filled the

street. Mencken couldn't tell who they were coming from or directed at. He leapt from the car, searching for Rosie. Had she fired? Had she been fired at? He wasn't sure. Then he saw her, running toward the two women at the gym door. Fear mixed with relief in his gut. He looked to his right as saw the boy running back to the car. A man also dressed in black stood at the driver's side door. He appeared to be disassembling some sort of rifle. When the boy arrived at the car, the man tossed the pieces of the rifle down a gutter grate next to the car. Both assailants got back in the car.

Mencken ran across the street to Rosie. All three women were on the ground. Anita was lying down. Rosie and the other woman knelt beside her. The kneeling woman was crying. Rosie's hands were interlocked, pressing hard into Anita's shoulder. Blood seeped between her fingers.

"You alright?" Mencken said to Rosie.

"I'm fine," she barked. "Call 9-1-1."

Mencken stood and reached for his phone. As he did, the old car passed them slowly. The assailant in the ski mask looked out at the scene. With a finger, he made a gun and pretended to shoot Mencken. Mencken snapped a picture of the car's licenses plate number before dialing.

Hours later, they climbed the steps of their apartment building. After waiting for the ambulance to leave, and then answering questions about what they'd seen, Rosie and Mencken were finally home.

Mencken paused at her door to tell Rosie goodnight, but Rosie kept walking. "Oh no," she said. "You owe me coffee. Take me on a stake out with no coffee or snacks. I was shot at. I at least get coffee."

When they arrived at Mencken's door, he reached for his keys, but before he could retrieve them, Rosie pulled a small lock pick kit from her pocket and went to work. She had the door open in seconds. Stepping aside, she motioned with her arm for him to step through.

"Well, thank you, ma'am," Mencken said with false formality.

Rosie laughed. "You need to replace these shitty locks," she said. "I keep waiting for you to take the hint."

Mencken walked over to his sink, opened the cabinet to the right and removed two glasses.

"I'll just have mine black," Rosie called, sitting on his bed, admiring the map on the wall.

Mencken brought over the glasses and a bottle of whiskey. "After tonight, you get the good stuff."

Rosie laughed. "We need to change your interpretation of 'good stuff'," she said as she took the drink. "Hey," she said with surprise. "What's that?"

Mencken turned to look at the tree of Cabal hierarchy painted on the wall behind him. On top of the question mark, over the word "hitman", was a white, lined, piece of paper. It was held to the wall by a small knife jammed into the drywall. Mencken reached up and pulled the knife out. It was heavy. Its grip was warm. From the tip, he withdrew the note.

"Don't touch it, dumbass," Rosie snapped, leaping to her feet. "You're contaminating evidence."

Mencken opened the note and read it aloud. "Congratulations. You have our full attention."

Rosie held out a plastic bag she obtained from the kitchen. "Drop it in here," she said. "No sleep tonight. I've got prints and a license plate to run."

CHAPTER TEN

Menken's alarm failed to wake him. It was after ten before he rolled out of bed, which was fine since there was nothing on the calendar for the day. He looked in the fridge, but it was barren. He tried to remember the last time he'd been shopping. Throwing on an old t-shirt and jeans, he headed toward Imani's.

It had been a late night for Mencken. After finding the knife and the note, Rosie had run off in search of clues. He'd then stayed up writing until close to two in the morning. Fueled by the evening's events and the threatening note, Mencken had become a fire hydrant, articles and blog posts rushed from his fingers. He finished a piece on Anita Dickson called "The Savior of Perkins in Critical Care." He cranked out two more for his blog. The first called, "The Night We Stopped the Knife," and the second "Baltimore's Very Own Organized Crime." And there was a fourth, "Rosario Jiminez: The Bravest Woman I Know." That one he held in his documents folder, unpublished. It was too personal, too revealing to share with the world. Before falling asleep, he'd called Rosie and ran his new plan by her.

The normal brunch crew was in the bar. Spencer sat to

the left of the door, sipping coffee and pointing to everyone who looked at him. At the table next to him were two other homeless men Mencken had seen panhandling around the neighborhood. A twenty-something pastor with a thick red beard had taken up residence in the front by one of the windows. His laptop was open and he was hammering through email. Mencken nodded. He smiled and waved back. Abby was behind the counter looking as stunning as ever in a green apron. On anyone else, it would have looked dirty and worn. You might have offered to buy a new one for someone wearing it, but Abby made it look like it belonged in the newest Victoria Secret catalog. Imani, today in a black tank top and silver-gray camouflage pants, was cooking a massive amount of pancakes. Mencken took in the room, enjoying the predictability of it all.

Not everyone was a regular, though. There were four people who stood out. The first was a young African-American man talking to Abby. He was dressed to kill: gray slacks, a crisp button-down with the sleeves rolled up, and a black suit vest. Every item seemed to be tailored specifically for the young man. Mencken was most impressed by his shoes. They were black and shiny, without a scuff in sight.

The strangers were sitting at Mencken's table in the back of the room. The odd looking trio comprised of a giant weightlifter dressed in black, and two petite college-aged girls dressed in white t-shirts and blue sweat pants.

Mencken's curiosity demanded that he speak to all of them. Looking at the group and the young man, he decided to tackle Abby's friend first because the suit seemed a more promising conversational partner than the weightlifter.

"Hey Abby," Mencken said. She and the new guy were leaning into each other, like two school girls sharing secrets.

She straightened up, "Good morning. What can I get

you?"

Mencken extended his hand to the man in the suit. "Mencken Cassie," Mencken said.

The man swiveled on his stool to face Mencken. His eyes were a beautiful hazel that, in contrast to his dark skin, seemed to shine. "Hunter Stockton," he said, shaking Mencken's hand.

"I need breakfast, Abby," Mencken said. "Tell Imani to surprise me."

"Another order of pancakes," Abby yelled over her shoulder.

"Got it," Imani called.

"Anything else?" Abby asked.

"Coffee?" Mencken said. Abby turned to fill a mug for him. "So," Mencken said to the suit. "How do you two know each other?"

Abby returned with the full mug. "Hunter works for my dad," she said.

"For almost a full year now," he said, grinning at her.

"What do you do for him?" Mencken said.

"I'm kind of like his personal assistant. I do whatever needs to be done."

Mencken didn't know what kind of business Abby's father was in, but whatever it was, it must pay well. "What'd you do before you came to work for Abby's dad?"

"About four years ago," Abby answered. "Daddy met Hunter, saw potential in him, and sent him to school in Europe."

"Wow," Mencken said. "Tell me about that."

"Not much to tell," Hunter said. "She makes it sound more exciting than it is. I was a poor kid living on the West Side. Our paths crossed, and Mr. Deces took a chance on me."

Mencken sipped his coffee, intrigued by the story. "What did you study overseas?"

"A little bit of everything," Hunter said. "It was more

like an apprenticeship than a traditional school. I went to live with a man Mr. Deces respected and wanted me to model. I patterned myself after him."

"That's very," Mencken struggled to find an example, "ancient Greek? Like students and the feet of Plato?"

"Yeah," Hunter laughed. "If Plato was an angry Frenchman, then sure."

"So," Mencken said, sipping his coffee again, "does her father know you're dating?"

"That's none of your business," Abby said, angrily.

"Very perceptive," Hunter replied. "We haven't told him, but I'm sure he knows. He knows everything."

Abby shrugged. "No use fighting it. Nothing hides from Daddy's eyes." It sounded to Mencken as if she were quoting something , but he didn't know what, probably a family saying of some sort.

"Speaking of," Hunter said, standing. "I should go." Extending his hand to Mencken he said, "Mr. Cassie, it's nice to meet the man behind the newspaper articles."

Mencken's chest swelled with pride. It's the first time someone he didn't know recognized his name. "Pleasure to meet you too, Mr. Stockton," Mencken said, shaking Hunter's hand with excitement. Wanting to give the couple a private goodbye, he grabbed his coffee and headed to the table in the back.

The odd trio was sitting in silence. The giant bodybuilder sat with this arms crossed and his eyes closed. The two women sat across from each other. They were playing cards, some sort dueling solitaire. Mencken pulled out the chair across from the giant and sat down. "Mencken Cassie," he said. "Do you mind if I join you?"

"Yes," the giant said. His voice was deep and rough as if a bulldog was growling somewhere deep in his throat. Mencken couldn't place his accent or the letters tattooed on his forearms. Whatever language it was, the thick, swirling script looked beautiful. He wore a thick, long curly, black beard that matched his tight fitting black t-shirt. In stark contrast, his head was shaved and tan. In total, the man was quite a spectacle

The woman to Mencken's right put down her cards and looked up at Mencken. Her blonde hair was cut in a wavy bob. She had bright blue eyes that were a perfect match for her pale complexion. "I'm Melody," she said. "This is my partner, Agnew."

The second woman, an olive-skinned lady whose brown hair was pulled back into a ponytail, held out her hand to Mencken, "My first name is Rachel, but everyone calls me Agnew."

Mencken shook her hand and then looked at the bodybuilder. "And you are?"

The man's eyes opened like ancient doors in need of oiling. The deep brown pools took Mencken in, and then closed again. The weightlifter's arms looked as if they were filled with rocks. Each muscle was defined and well used. The shirt he wore stretched tight around his pectoral muscles, revealing their impressive definition.

"That's Rothman," Melody said.

"What brings you all to Imani's?" Mencken asked leaning back in his chair.

With his arms still crossed and eyes still closed, Rothman grunted.

"We're friends of Chris and Jose," Agnew interpreted. "Do you know them?"

"Imani introduced us a few days ago," Mencken said. "How do you know them?"

"We share common interests," Rothman grumbled.

"We're kind of related," Melody said. "How do you know Imani?"

"I'm a regular. This is my office," Mencken replied with pride.

The giant mumbled something under his breath Mencken couldn't make out.

"Alright everyone," Imani said, arriving with a tray of plates and mugs. "Breakfast is here." She set the tray on the table next to her, passed plates with three pancakes and normal sized mugs of coffee to Mencken, Melody, and Agnew. Then, in front of Rothman, she placed a larger plate with ten pancakes and a beer mug filled to the brim with coffee.

Rothman opened his eyes and uncrossed his arms. He took Imani's hands in his own. They swallowed her hands completely. "Thank you, Ms. Imani. You are very kind." Then he released her and cut into all ten pancakes with his knife.

"No problem," Imani said. "I'm just glad you made the trip."

"Where'd you come from?" Mencken asked.

"We're from Philly," Melody said. "We got a call from Chris this morning, so we came down."

"Is everything alright?" Mencken asked, feigning concern.

"It's just a family thing," Agnew said, her mouth stuffed with pancakes. "These are great by the way," she told Imani.

"Thanks, sweetie," Imani replied.

"What about you?" Mencken said to Rothman. "You from Philadelphia too?"

Rothman stared at Mencken with disgust. Then looking at Agnew he said, "Information and knowledge are assets to be preserved, not served from the street corner to every passerby."

"Don't lecture me, big boy," Agnew snapped back. "I'm only here as a favor to Chris. I don't want or need your shit."

"So not from Philly," Mencken said.

The giant looked at Imani and asked, "What did the small Jose say of this one?"

Imani sipped her coffee and smiled at Mencken. "That he was undecided."

"Interesting," Melody said.

"What's interesting?" Mencken asked. "What does that

mean?"

"It's not a good thing," Agnew answered. "But I guess it could be worse."

"It means that knowledge of The Rothman is not for your consumption," Rothman said with disinterest.

Mencken's cell phone buzzed in his pocket. It was a text from Rosie: Nothing on the knife or note. They're clean. Plate on the car came back stolen. Second dead end. Captain said he will give us ten minutes to share your plan. Come now.

Mencken stood. "It was great to meet all of you. Sorry. I've got to run. Something important just came up."

CHAPTER ELEVEN

The text seemed promising. Mencken checked it again to make sure he was in the right place. @BmoreVoice something huge going down at Exeter and Fawn. Get there fast.

He looked at the street signs to his right. It was the right place. He had always known someday Twitter would betray him. There'd been the occasional troll, but mostly he'd only received good leads from the medium. His luck was bound to run out at some point.

He pulled his bike to the curb, popped the kickstand, and stepped off. The street was quiet. Rowhomes in all directions. Fawn was a beautiful street. At one end was the downtown skyline. At the other, there was a distant outline of Hopkins Hospital. Mencken allowed himself a moment to enjoy the towering buildings. He closed his eyes and tried to picture all the people moving in them. Thousands upon thousands of people, going about their lives, with no knowledge of his existence. Something he planned to remedy. When this was all over and the Cabal was sunk, they'd know his name. Mencken Cassie – Savior of the City.

He checked the text again. It had been sent by

@Friend76201. Not promising. He checked the profile. This was the only tweet the account had sent. He thought about replying. Would a sharp retort only invite more of this nonsense?

He looked around again. There was no one on the street. No cars passing by. At each point of the intersection there were small businesses: two bars, a barbershop, and a print shop. All four had hand-painted signs over their doors. It was classic old Baltimore. No bright lights. No neon. Just withering wooden signs. Mencken checked the time on his phone. He decided to give it another few minutes.

He took out his phone and tweeted back. @Friend76201 I'm here. Nothing happening.

An immediate reply came through. @BmoreVoice Wait for it.

"Sounds ominous," Mencken said to himself.

Mencken sat on his bike. He flipped his backpack around, unzipped the top, and took out the ham sandwich he'd made that morning. After meeting with Rosie's captain yesterday, he'd finally found time to go to the grocery store. He withdrew the sandwich from the bag, looked around again, and took a bite.

Later, Mencken would struggle to remember what came first: the rush of wind, the loud boom, or the heat of the flames. They all seemed to happen at once as the bars on opposing corners erupted like volcanos. The force threw Mencken and his bike to the ground. Car windshields shattered. Alarms sounded. The orange, yellow, and blue flames engulfed the corner rowhomes in waves, consuming the buildings and spreading to their next-door neighbors.

Mencken sat up and tried to get his bearings. His ears rang and his head pounded. The heat of the flames scorched his skin and burned his eyes, forcing them closed. He found his phone in his pocket. Coughing, he squinted and dialed 9-1-1.

"9-1-1 operator, how can I help you?"

Mencken forced his voice into a controllable tone. "There's a," his voice was caught by the heat of the flames. "There's a giant fire," he forced. "At Exeter and Fawn. Send lots of trucks. You'll need them all." Then he hung up.

He knew he needed to move. He couldn't stay between the two fires. He grabbed his bike by the handlebars and struggled to stand it up. Looking left and right, he tried to figure out his next move.

A car was approaching. It flew toward Mencken at an alarming pace. Mencken wondered if it were some kind of first responder, but then realizing it was just an old clunker, he popped the kickstand on his bike and waved his hands, hoping to warn the car off.

It continued toward him, not slowing. Mencken waved again, but the car persisted. Afraid he was going to be run over, Mencken grabbed his bike and pushed it toward the curb that wasn't on fire.

The car flew through the intersection and made a hard right turn. The tires screeched. Rubber skidded across asphalt leaving long black lines on the fading pavement. Had he not been surrounded by an inferno, Mencken would have found the driver's skill impressive.

As the car's back wheels fishtailed passed him, the rear driver's side door came open and something flew from the car. It was big and brown. It rolled a few times and then came to stop. Mencken ran to where it had landed. It was large and soft, wrapped in a brown, cloth shell. Fighting his inner urge to flee the heat, he grabbed the cloth and pulled it back, revealing its contents.

The sight of what was wrapped in the brown sheet sent Mencken into shock. He scrambled backward with his hands and feet, desperate to escape it. At the same time, transfixed by the horror of it, Mencken couldn't take his eyes off the cloth's contents. In the sheet was the beaten body of Anita Dickson. Her nose had been smashed.

Where her eyes should have been there were hollow sockets, but despite the disfigurement, Mencken knew it was her.

He felt tears in his eyes. He turned, and vomited to the left. Bits of ham sandwich and yellow stomach acid lingered in his mouth. Staggering to his feet, he stumbled to his bike. He could hear the sirens coming in the distance. He kicked down on the ignition and his bike roared to life. Willing himself under control, he sped away.

Although Mencken wouldn't read it until later, as he sped off his phone buzzed again. @Bmorevoice Do you enjoy having my attention? More to come. Insert chapter ten text here. Insert chapter ten text here.

CHAPTER TWELVE

"You ready?" Mencken asked Tay.

Tay held a large, cordless, video camera on his shoulder. His baseball cap was turned backward. Over his left shoulder was a bag holding the audio equipment for Mencken's wireless microphone. "We could just do this with a cellphone camera. You know that right?" said Tay, frustrated by the weight of the equipment. "You didn't have to make me haul all this shit out here."

"The gear is intimidating," Mencken replied, looking at the house across the street. "It lends authenticity, and it'll distract him."

"Oh, you mean because in real life I'm currently out-of-work cameraman hoping to pick up the next movie that rolls into town, and you're a blogger. Is that what you mean? Distract him from the fact that we have no business being here or doing this? Why didn't you just call some real reporters?"

"Two things," Mencken replied. He rolled the wireless microphone between his hands. "First, I'm a journalist, a real journalist. Not a blogger. Second, I don't care who he thinks we are. I need him distracted from his urge to shoot us both in the face."

"I love hanging out with you," Tay said flatly. "It's the best."

Mencken studied the house across the street. It had two stories, with a wrap-around front porch. The white siding and blue shutters made it look peaceful, like a place you'd like to spend a weekend relaxing. There was even a hammock hanging between the two large oaks that shaded most of the front lawn.

"You ready?" Mencken asked.

"I didn't drive out to the 'burbs for fun," Tay replied. "I'll start taping when we cross the street. We can edit out everything you don't want later. Just put the microphone in his face. It's all he'll see."

"Let's do this," Mencken said.

The two comrades-in-arms crossed the street. The house was surrounded by a waste-high white picket fence. Mencken reached over and undid the latch of the gate. He took the lead up the cobblestone path to the front door. He paused before knocking, asking himself if this was something he really wanted to do. Then he remembered the heat of the fire. He remembered how it had licked his skin. He remembered Anita Dickson's missing eyes. He remembered the note in his apartment, and the pictures of him sleeping. This was war. It was already too late to turn back. Shots had been fired. Hesitation would lead to death.

Mencken grabbed the brass door knocker and hammered on the door. "Get ready," he told Tay.

"Ready to run," Tay replied under his breath.

Mencken wasn't prepared for who opened the door. A little girl in pink footy pajamas stood before them. She welcomed Mencken with an unimpressed scowl. Two braids sprouted from the sides of her hair. "Hello," she said.

Mencken bent down to her level. "What's your name?" he said.

"Antonia Electra Robertson," the little girl said with a smile.

Mencken appreciated the intentional Greek reference in the girl's middle name. In the Greek legend, Agamemnon had six kids, one of whom was a daughter named Electra. "Is your daddy here?" Mencken asked.

The little girl said sweetly, "One minute please." Then she turned and screamed with all her might, "Daaad!" She turned back to Mencken and said, "He'll be right here." Then she skipped away, disappearing into the house.

The man who came down the stairs was frighteningly fit. His pectorals and biceps were clearly defined beneath the blue Under Armour top he wore. It was contrasted by flowing, blue sweatpants, and black leather house shoes. His hair was graying, and he wore black-rimmed eyeglasses. He looked as though he had been in the middle of curling up with a great novel.

Confusion rose on the man's face when he saw the camera. "Can I help you?" he asked hesitantly.

"Yes, sir," Mencken said, speaking into the microphone. "My name is Mencken Cassie." Mencken made note that there was no recognition on the man's face when he heard Mencken's name. This could mean the man had never heard of him, or it could mean that he was gifted at keeping his cards close to his chest. "I'm a reporter," Mencken finished.

"I think you have the wrong house," the man said, starting to close the door.

Mencken jammed his foot in the way, forcing the door open. "Are you Anthony Robertson, sir?" he said, holding out the microphone.

The man was not mesmerized by the microphone as Tay had predicted. Rather, he locked eyes with Mencken. His glare was powerful made Mencken want to step back. The man said again, "Listen, you've got the wrong-"

Mencken interrupted, "Are you the Anthony Robertson who goes by the alias Agamemnon?"

The man laughed and gave a warm smile to the camera. "I have no idea what you are talking about. I'm sorry. Like

I said, you have the wrong house."

He pushed the door again, but Mencken held firm. Although Mencken couldn't match Agamemnon in fitness, he had six inches on him, and therefore would be difficult to move without more excessive force.

Tay moved to the right, ensuring he could see around Mencken with the camera.

"Mr. Robertson, are you the owner of 2424 Pinewood Ave, 2555 Garrison Boulevard, 1850 North Ave, and 792 Bridgewater Road?"

"Alright," the man said with intensifying force. Rage flashed behind his eyes. "That' enough. We're done. You should go."

"Were you aware, sir, that all of those homes are being used to facilitate sex-trafficking?"

"I said that's enough," the man growled, pushing the microphone away.

"Are you also aware, that-" Mencken paused, listening to a cell phone ringing somewhere in the house. He smiled. Agamemnon looked back toward it, his concentration briefly interrupted. Mencken continued, "Are you also aware, sir, that a Baltimore City Police division is simultaneously raiding all four of those properties as we speak? In fact," Mencken added with glee. "I bet that phone call is from one of your crew."

With one swift move, placing both his hands on Mencken's chest, Agamemnon threw Mencken to the floor. Then, with the speed of a viper, he leapt forward and snatched the camera from Tay. In fear, Tay backed away, almost falling down the porch steps.

Agamemnon threw the camera inside his house. It shattered to pieces as it hit the marble tile of the entryway. He then moved back to the front door and kicked Mencken in the jaw, sending the taller man back onto the floor of the porch. Before Mencken could resist, Agamemnon was sitting on his chest, with his hands around Mencken's throat.

"You must be some special kind of stupid," Agamemnon said softly, "to come to my house with this shit."

Mencken tried to speak, but he couldn't get enough air to form words. His mind began to race. Reflexively, he grabbed Agamemnon's hands, but they didn't budge. Panic rose in Mencken's heart. His eyes darted left and right, desperate for help.

"To my home," Agamemnon said again. "To my fucking home." With a sharp jolt, he lifted Mencken's head and slammed it into the porch. Mencken could feel his brain rattling in his skull.

Agamemnon released his grip from Mencken's throat. Mencken gasped for air. Agamemnon stood, and looked around. A neighbor two doors down, an elderly man in a t-shirt, came out of his garage with a lawn mower. Agamemnon waved. "Hey Charlie," he called. "If you hold up, I'll help you with that."

Mencken rose to one knee. He rubbed his aching neck. The world was still spinning around him. Slowly, he stood. Trying to control his pace, he calmly left the front porch. Agamemnon snickered, watching Mencken go. "Don't come back, you little shit," Agamemnon said.

Once out of arms reach, Mencken turned and replied, "We'll send you a bill for the camera. And tell your friends, I'm coming for all of you. I'm going to burn your little party to the ground."

Agamemnon laughed a belly laugh as if he'd been told the greatest joke in history. He leaned against his doorframe. "That's fantastic. The little no-name shit is threatening me. You're fucking hysterical."

"And tell your little hitman friend," Mencken added. "That he's at the top of my list. His days of freedom are numbered."

Agamemnon stopped laughing and looked at Mencken with earnest confusion. "You really have no idea who you're fucking with, do you?" Mencken saw fear behind his eyes, real fear.

"And tell him to stay the fuck out of my apartment," Mencken added as he walked away.

"Dead man walking," Agamemnon yelled to the neighborhood as Mencken left. "Hey little shit," he called as Mencken got in Tay's car. "Don't you fucking ever come to my house again."

CHAPTER THIRTEEN

Mencken was an unstoppable force. The words flowed through his hands. The dinner rush had come and gone. The evening drinkers had finished their cocktails. The night-cappers had called it and headed home. But he was a rock, unceasingly writing, despite the river of people flowing around him. He described in detail the raids on each brothel. He drew the connections to the original gangster, tracing the path of money back to Anthony Robertson. Mencken was going to reveal to the world the real face of the suburban dad. Embarrassing politicians was one thing, but like flowers that die at the end of a season, they were replaceable. For the first time, Mencken felt he was striking a lasting blow against the Cabal. He was taking down one of the inner circle, and it felt great.

"You need to pack it up," Imani said, knocking on the table with her fist.

Mencken didn't look up from his laptop. "I just need like, another hour," he said. "I'm starting the most important part."

"No," Imani said. "Now. You need to go now."

Mencken didn't stop typing. "Come on. You've never kicked me out before. What's the big deal?"

Imani marched to the wall behind him. "Leave, Mencken," said demanded as she yanked his laptop's power cord out of the wall socket.

Nothing happened. "Battery's charged," he said. "Thanks."

Imani slammed both her hands on his table. Mencken looked up for the first time. Her brow was furloughed with stress lines. "You need to go," she commanded.

"Is everything okay?" he asked, not remembering a time she had ever been this agitated.

She threw her hands in the air with exasperation. "Jesus, Mencken. It's one o'clock in the morning. I closed an hour ago."

"Wow," he said. He smiled proudly. "One? Really?" He started scanning his papers, checking his word count.

"I'm being serious," she pleaded. "You've got to go. They're coming back. You can't be here. I should have kicked you out an hour ago."

He looked up, his eyes glowing like a kid who'd just learned he was going to the circus. "I've cranked out over twelve thousand words today. Isn't that crazy? That's the start to a book."

Imani sat down across from him and looked him in the eyes. "Please. You have to leave."

Mencken leaned back in his chair and folded his arms. "Who's coming back?" he said.

"What?" Imani said, shaking her head.

"You said they are coming back. Who? Who's coming back? And why can't I be here."

"You just can't," she said, her head hung low. "Please leave."

Mencken and Imani were jerked from their conversation by a commotion at the front door. Jose flung the glass doors open. His white shirt was covered in red and black splotches. He was sweaty and pale like he'd run a marathon with no water. His eyes were red and bloodshot, and he was crying. "Imani," the young boy said softly through tears. "We need bandages."

Imani leapt to her feet, knocking her chair over behind her. "What happened?" There was fear in her voice. Mencken had never heard fear in Imani's voice.

Jose held the door open. Chris and Agnew entered next. Imani mumbled, "Oh thank Jesus," as Chris walked through the door.

Chris' mouth was a thin line. His eyes radiated fury. His yellow polo was as stained as Jose's. His right pants leg was torn at his calf.

Agnew had her left arm around Chris' shoulders. She was soaked in blood. The thick, red liquid oozed from a rip in the thigh of her blue sweatpants. Her face was streaked with it. It was matted in her hair. Like Jose, her eyes were bloodshot and she was crying.

"Agnew needs first aid," Chris said to Imani.

Imani shot up the stairs.

Chris sat Agnew in a chair in the middle of the room. He took two steps back and began to pace back and forth, muttering to himself.

Jose put his back against the wall and sank to the floor. Burying his head in his knees, he began to sob softly to himself.

The door pushed open again, and the giant Rothman ducked under the door frame. His face was a mix of rage and pain. There was a bloody scratch on his right shoulder. He went to one knee by Agnew's side and applied pressure to her wound with his hands. Agnew shrieked in pain.

"She fought bravely," Rothman said. The low rumble of his deep voice filled the room. Agnew wailed in response.

Imani appeared with what looked like a fishing tackle box. She ran to Rothman's side.

"I need something to clean the wound, a needle, and thread," he said. He took his blood-soaked hands off Agnew's leg and the blood began to ooze again. "It's just a minor wound," he explained to no one in particular.

"You're going to be fine. The Rothman has repaired much worse." He ripped her pants with his bare hands, exposing the wound. Imani opened the box, digging in the bottom, she retrieved the supplies and passed Rothman heavy gauze pads and a bottle of alcohol wash.

"I need a drink," Agnew said through tears.

Chris vaulted over the bar, grabbed a bottle of whiskey, hopped back over, and handed the bottle to Agnew. She took the screw cap off with her teeth and took a long swig.

Rothman blotted the gash with the gauze and rinsed it with the alcohol. After repeating the action three times, he'd cleared away much of the dried blood. "Once, when The Rothman was in Cairo," he said with very no expression as he threaded the needle Imani had given him, "the Gracanjo lost his leg. Cut off clean at the knee." He began to stitch Agnew's leg. She screamed through gritted teeth and took another swig from the bottle.

"All I had to repair him up was his sword and a campfire." He stitched more. Agnew yelled again. "I pressed the red hot blade against his wound and seared it closed. He lived. This is nothing like that. "

"Not helping, Rothman," Chris yelled. "Keep the damn stories to yourself."

"It is best she have something to keep her mind from the operation at hand," Rothman retorted.

A realization struck Imani. "Where's… Where's Melody?" she asked.

"She's dead," Agnew said, and then she took another long swig of the whiskey.

"Oh no," Imani muttered.

"Her body is in the trunk," Agnew said to no one in particular. "In the middle of the fight, they… They ripped her head off."

Jose's crying increased.

"Oh Jesus," Imani said.

"She died as we all should," Rothman said. "As a warrior, in the heat of battle."

Chris spun toward the empty side of the room, moving like a mama bear who'd heard her cubs cry. He pointed toward the darkness and screamed, "He's here!"

"Let him be," Rothman said.

Agnew cried in pain again as Rothman pulled the thread tight.

Ignoring the command, Chris moved across the room, knocking over chairs and tables in his path. His eyes filled with tears. A guttural cry escaped his lips. Arriving at the spot where he had been pointing, he began kicking the air and screaming, "Leave! You bastard! Leave!" In a frantic rage, he completed a powerful spin kick, dropping his heal into the wood floor with a crash. Back on his feet, he punched and the floor with both hands, like a boxer going at a punching bag. As he beat the invisible enemy, he screamed over and over, "Leave us alone! Leave us alone!"

Mencken watched in horror as Chris battled an invisible enemy, unsure of what to fear more: the insanity of the man who attacked shadows, or the precision and power of the wild man's assault.

Rothman completed the final stitch and tied the thread, and cut it with his teeth. "Finished," he said, admiring his handy handiwork.

Agnew took another swig of the whiskey. "You better go get him," she said to Imani, "before he tears up your floors."

Imani jumped to life. Running over to Chris, she moved to stand in front of him. Holding her hands up defensively, she said, "Baby. Baby. Look at me. Look here. Look at me baby."

Chris's assault slowed. He delivered a few more strikes, and then dropped to his knees. Tears overcame him and began to weep. "He's not supposed to be here," he moaned. "He's not supposed to follow us."

Imani came to him. She wrapped her arms around him. Rubbing his back she said, "Come on Baby. Let's go downstairs. He can't see you downstairs."

She and Chris stood together. "She was so young," Chris said. "She didn't have to go like that. She was so young. They tore her head off. They just…"

Imani supported his weight and rubbed his back as they walked. Holding each other, they moved passed Mencken to the basement stairs and disappeared in the darkness.

"Now you need to rest," Rothman said as he stood and stretched his shoulders, rolling them in circles. Agnew took another swig from the bottle.

Mencken realized at that moment that his mouth was hanging open. He looked to the young woman and her newly bandaged wound. He watched as the giant took a swig from her bottle. He looked at Jose, who had stopped crying, but was still sitting on the floor with his knees clutched to his chest. Finally, the moment overtook him. Questions rushed to Mencken's mind. Words stuttered from his mouth. He rose to his feet, but the only question that would fall from his lips was, "What the fuck is going on?"

Rothman, Agnew, and Jose all looked in his direction with surprise. None of them had noticed him until that moment.

"And what the fuck happened to Melody?" Mencken demanded. "And why are you bleeding? And why the fuck is Chris losing his mind? What the fuck is going on?"

Rothman crossed the room with frightening determination. With his left hand, the giant took Mencken by the neck and lifted the reporter off the ground. Mencken's feet dangled in the air. His hands tore at Rothman's arm like a kitten scratching at steel. Mencken's mind raced as his lungs begged for air.

Rothman spoke softly. Each word was like the steady drum of a blacksmith's hammer. "Small man," the giant said, applying more pressure to Mencken's neck. "You will not disgrace this ground with vile language or lack of respect for the fallen."

Mencken tried to speak, tried to scream, tried to force any sound from his throat, but all he could do was wheeze for air.

"Your witness of this time was unfortunate. Now I must bring this to an end," Rothman said.

Mencken's eyes grew wide with panic.

Jose stood and yelled, "No! No more death tonight."

Rothman loosened his grip. "He has no place here," he said.

"Put him down," the teen commanded. "This is my city. You are my guest. And I say enough people have died."

Rothman sneered at Mencken. Then, lowering his arm slowly, he dropped Mencken to the floor. Mencken fell to his knees and held his neck with both hands. He gasped for breath, trying to regain control of his senses.

Rothman turned his back on the reporter. "He is yours to clean up then," he said to Jose, "He will not be here when I return. If he is, I will forget that I am a guest." The giant walked over to Agnew and said, "Come. You must rest." He knelt down beside her, slid arms under her, and effortlessly picked her up. Then the two of them disappeared into the basement.

Jose crossed the room to Mencken's table. He closed Mencken's laptop, placed it in Mencken's backpack, and zipped the pack up. He then walked over to Mencken and held it out for Mencken to take.

"What happened?" Mencken said, finally catching his breath again.

"There were more of them than we expected. They flanked us. Things went south," Jose said. "And then... Our lines broke down, and they got Melody. We had to retreat"

Mencken stood and took his bag. He looked Jose up and down. He thought back to the stakeout at the gym. He thought of the Sahib's story about the assault at the park. He thought about the recovery house and the black puddle on the ground. "You don't lose often, do you?" Mencken said, accusingly.

Jose cocked his head to the left. "No. We don't."

Mencken took his bag. Slinging it over his right shoulder, he said, "I see you now."

Jose sighed. "I don't know what you think you know, but-"

Mencken cut him off. "I'm on to you and I'm coming. Game time is over, because I know your secret. You can't hide anymore."

"You don't understand. We were protecting the city tonight," Jose said, rubbing his head with his hands.

Mencken laughed. "Is that how Chris has brainwashed you? Tell yourself whatever you need to, kid. I know the truth. I know who you are."

Jose stood up a chair Chris had knocked over and took a seat in it. "I'm too tired for this tonight. You weren't supposed to be here."

Mencken strode proudly to the front door. Before leaving, he turned and said, "But I was. And now I know the whole story."

CHAPTER FOURTEEN

The streets were quiet. At two in the morning, nothing on this side of town was awake. The neighborhoods in northern Baltimore still showed signs of the suburbs they were originally designed to be. While the main commercial streets felt like city, but the residential areas between them contained standalone houses with yards, driveways, and garages. Nevertheless, all the city's problems were present: rats, crime, drugs, a struggling education system. They were just a little less condensed.

Mencken knew who the tweet was from the minute it had come in. The hitman and his child partner were punching back. Mencken almost hadn't come. He was terrified of what he would find. Would more buildings explode? Would more bodies by thrown from cars? Or maybe this was it? Maybe he'd gone too far? Coordinating the takedown of Agamemnon's brothels had to have at least dented the Cabal's revenue. Maybe they'd tired of the game and it was Mencken's turn to have his eyes dug out? He'd tried to go back to bed, but his curiosity wouldn't allow it. He had to know what they were summoning him to see.

He killed the engine of his bike in front of the house.

He'd recognized the address right away. It was the residence of the State's Attorney in Baltimore, Alexander Cleveland. The up-and-coming lawyer lived here with his wife and sixteen-month-old son. Mencken had done a piece on the Clevelands after Alexander was elected last year. Alexander and his wife, Tamara, had sat in their living room with Mencken for an hour. It'd been a fluff piece. No hard questions, but Mencken felt he'd gotten a sense of the couple. They were good people, who cared about the city and were trying to carve out a life in it.

Mencken held tight to his handlebars. He didn't want to get off his bike. He didn't want to know what horrors lay inside.

Cars were sprinkled through the street. Mencken looked up and down the block and then took a deep breath, rallying his courage. Stepping off his bike, he faced the house. It was red brick and beautifully landscaped – nothing fancy, but everything was in place. Purple flowers bloomed in a flowerbed located under a large picture window. The shades were drawn, but the lights were on.

The front door was located on the left-hand side of the house. Mencken walked up the driveway, onto the small brick porch. He wasn't sure if he should knock or ring the doorbell. What was the protocol for the middle of the night? And what would he say when Alexander answered the door?

"Hey, remember me? Mencken Cassie? Here's the deal. I know it's the middle of the night, but there's this hitman? And, well, he and I are at war with each other. So he gave me your address on Twitter tonight and told me to come here. Have you, maybe, seen him?" Yeah. This was going to go great.

Mencken sighed. He reached out to knock on the door, but before making contact with the wood, he noticed the door was already cracked. He paused and considered leaving, just walking away. He could call Rosie. Give her the address. Then she could tell him what was inside. He looked at his shoes. If he left, when he looked in the mirror tomorrow, who would look back at him?

He pushed the door softly. It swung open. Alexander was there to greet him. The State's Attorney lay on the floor, in a pool of blood. Dressed in comfortable house clothes, he rested unmoving, on his stomach, facing the living room, his bare feet were inches from the swing of the door.

Mencken thought through the scene. Alexander had answered the door and then turned his back on the guest. Had he known the person, or had they said something to make him turn? There was an open wound at the base of his neck, and three or four more in his back. Around each incision, circles of blood pulled the State's Attorney's white undershirt tight to his skin.

Mencken looked down the short hallway. He knew there was more. He knew this wasn't the end. Moving gently, trying not to touch anything or disturb the scene in any way, Mencken made his way past the dead State's Attorney.

Passing the entrance to the kitchen, Mencken stepped into the living room. It was a spacious room with vaulted, wood ceilings. Straight ahead were stairs to the second-floor bedrooms. Mencken turned to face the giant, flat-screen television hung on the wall opposite him. Between the flat-screen and himself was a blue couch. On the couch was Mrs. Cleveland, unmoving, peaceful. Her reflection looked at him in the TV, but he couldn't raise his eyes to it. He couldn't bear for her to see him through the dark screen.

He stepped cautiously around the couch, keeping his eyes on his shoes. He could feel her looking at him. Her dead eyes following him as he circled her. Swallowing, he looked up and met her gaze.

Her mouth was open and her head hung back. Blood from her neck wound soaked the front of her green t-shirt, causing it to cling to her skin. Her hair was pulled into a ponytail. Like Anita Dickson, her eyes were missing. The caverns stared back at him. The insides of the sockets looked like dried, marinara-soaked sponges.

None of this mattered to Mencken. He couldn't dwell on any of it. All he could see was what was in her lap. Clutched tightly to her chest, sitting in her lap, covered in a mix of his mom's blood and his own, was the small, year-and-a-half old, Cleveland boy. The black handled knife that had been used to kill his parents protruded from his neck.

Vomit rose in Mencken's throat, and tears burned his eyes. He locked his jaw so none of the acidic spew would fall from his mouth and defile the scene with his weakness. He swallowed the vile liquid, thinking it would restore his confidence, but his legs grew instantly weak. He had to sit. He fell to the floor and looked at the mother and son. His face in his hands, he lost control of his emotions and wept. Howling like a child with a broken limb, he cried over the innocence lost and the love desecrated. What kind of monster would kill a mother and her infant son? Who were these people? Why? Why come into the house to slaughter the entire Cleveland family? What had the sixteen-month-old done to the Cabal?

Mencken lost time. He stared at the face of the young boy, an eternal cry on his lips. Mencken imagined the child screaming as his mother's grip tightened and then went limp. He imagined her sitting on the couch, in front of the monsters that would take her life, clutching her son, and whispering prayers. He could still smell her fear in the room. It hung in the air, haunting the space.

Mencken rose. He took out his phone and called 9-1-1, giving them the address. When they asked if he'd gone inside, he said "No. I only opened the door."

His second call was to Rosie. It was a short, tear-filled message with the address and a request that she "come quickly." He didn't know if she would get it in time. Surely, she was asleep.

Gently, Mencken gently navigated passed Alexander, making sure to leave no trace that he'd entered the Clevelands' home. Once on the front porch, he sat again, unable to stop replaying in his mind what he'd seen. The imagined cries of the young boy tore at his eardrums. Rattling in his mind, it refused to be silenced.

Mencken took a deep breath and forced away his tears. He stood again, wanting to walk, wanting to run, wanting to be away, to be anywhere but here. Down the street, something caught his eye. There was movement in the periphery, on his left. Mencken turned and peered into the night. He thought that, maybe, at the end of the street were people. Two people. Leaning against the hood of a car. He looked closer, rubbing his eyes, thinking he was imagining them, but he wasn't. It was them. Watching him.

Approaching sirens echoed in the background. Reinforcements were on their way.

The two figures are the end of the street stood, got in their car, and drove away.

A few minutes later, and another text came through:

@BmoreVoice Tag. You're it.

CHAPTER FIFTEEN

It had been a normal morning for John Hammerjam, the CEO of Rebuild Baltimore. He'd risen at five and jogged on his treadmill for an hour while watching the news on his large flat screen television. After his morning exercise, he'd enjoyed a fruit and cheese platter for breakfast, along with French-pressed coffee. As he ate, his assistant read the day's schedule to him and explained the emails she felt he needed to return.

After breakfast, he'd basked under the eight heads of his shower. Four above his head and four at his midsection, the soft spray enveloped his body from all angles. He hummed to himself as he scrubbed. The soap he used had been a gift from a woman he'd spent a few nights with last month. It was filled with tiny grains of sand, supposedly taken from an exotic island just before it had been swallowed by the Pacific.

Hammerjam chose a gray suit with a purple tie. He had a board meeting at two and needed to remind them that he was king. The deep purple would serve as well as any crown. It radiated power and wealth. He pulled tight the small, black laces of his hand-made shoes as he dictated an email to his assistant. It had been a normal morning for

John Hammerjam.

Mencken had been waiting outside the front door of the building for hours. He'd come there straight after leaving the Cleveland Carnage. That's what he'd decided to call it, "The Cleveland Carnage." He liked the alliteration of it. He'd said it over and over, holding the words in his mouth, tasting them. "Cleveland Carnage Cleveland Carnage Cleveland Carnage."

Mencken's eyes throbbed with exhaustion and dehydration. His beard was a combination of snot, tears, and vomit. His legs wobbled beneath him. There was only one thing he wanted more than sleep – to strike back.

He'd waited as the cops processed the scene. Three stretchers. Three body bags. Two large. One small. Watching the coroner's van silently roll away, Mencken had known he needed to hit fast and hard. He'd jumped on his bike and sped to the Rebuild Baltimore Headquarters, to wait for the CEO's arrival.

The second Hammerjam's chauffeur opened the door of the Town Car, Mencken pounced. He ran toward the car with his phone extended like a camera, yelling, "John Hammerjam! John Hammerjam! I need a statement." As he approached the car, regret-filled Mencken's mind. He didn't know what he would say to the executive. He wasn't prepared. He wished he'd had the forethought to call Tay, to tell him to bring a camera. He was forcing this.

Much to his shock, before reaching the door of the black town car, Mencken found himself falling backward, crashing into the concrete. The impact jarred his spine and made his tailbone sing with pain. It was only from this low position on the pavement that Mencken considered that the chauffeur might also double as a bodyguard.

John Hammerjam stood over Mencken. His shoes were freshly shined. The thin black laces were perfectly double-knotted into crisp bows. Mencken couldn't help but study them, as they were inches from his face.

"Can I help you?" the CEO said.

Mencken looked up. Seeing the man's smug smile buried his embarrassment and rekindled his rage. Mencken jumped to his feet. "I'm with the Star. I'm here for a statement from you on the death of State's Attorney Alexander Cleveland."

Standing, Mencken had inches on the man. Hammerjam looked up into Mencken's eyes. It was the look a cat gave a mouse right after the mouse had been caught, right before it had been eaten. "It's tragic. A great loss to the city. Alex was a good man. We will all mourn him."

"Will you? Will you really? My understanding is that he was building a case against you claiming the misappropriation of city monies."

"I'm not sure what you're talking about."

The file folders in Mencken's mind delivered a dagger of information. "The city awarded your company four million dollars fifteen months ago. For the improvement of infrastructure around your waterfront development in Canton. The State's Attorney was preparing to prove those funds were instead rolled into the redevelopment of the luxury apartments you're building in the Inner Harbor."

"I don't know anything about that," Hammerjam said, still smiling, still maintaining eye contact. "I'm not sure what you are insinuating, but Alex was a good friend. We often played squash together. He and his family were at my apartment last month for dinner. I'm going to miss him."

The verbal shot to Mencken's understanding left him breathless. He wasn't prepared for the idea of a personal relationship between the two men. The revelation made him tired. He shouldn't be here. He hadn't done enough homework.

"Are you okay? You don't look so well," Hammerjam said, still smiling.

Things started to spin. Mencken closed his eyes, but all he could hear was the imagined screaming of the dead Cleveland child.

Hammerjam grabbed the back of Mencken's neck and pulled Mencken's ear down to his mouth. "You're not with the Star. Not really. I know exactly who you are, and I know what's happening to you. The spinning you're feeling right now, the chaos, the mayhem in your mind – that's his true gift. And he's taken a shine to you."

Mencken tried to pull back, repulsed, but Hammerjam's grip was too strong. The shorter man held him tight, refusing to let him escape.

Hammerjam continued to smile and whisper, "He knows everything about you. It's how he works. There's a good chance you've even met him, or at least his disciples. They like to make personal contact before the hunt begins. They're like hounds that have your scent. You keep calling him a hitman, but he's not. He's much more. He's the Grimm Reaper. And he's coming for you. And once he tires of toying with you, he'll finish you off; that is, if he doesn't drive you mad first. Either way, you're already done."

Releasing his neck, Hammerjam pushed Mencken hard with both hands. The tall reporter fell to his butt once again. "Look at you," Hammerjam said, standing over Mencken. "Now look at me. You think you're even a speck on my radar? You don't even register as a threat." Laughing, Hammerjam walked away.

CHAPTER SIXTEEN

"I'm sorry, sir. He can't see you right now," the Baltimore Star receptionist said. She stood between Mencken and the entrance to the office. It was a brave move for the five-foot-two, hundred pound woman in a blue skirt and silk blouse.

"I need to talk to him, now!" Mencken yelled as he stomped his foot. "Right! Now!"

"Mr. Winchell is in a staff meeting, sir," the receptionist said, calmly. "I'll tell him you're here as soon as they are done. If you would just take a seat over-"

Mencken grabbed the small woman by the shoulders and pushed her out of his way. She squeaked with surprise as she fell. He didn't pause to see if she was okay. Storming through the door of the newspaper headquarters, he frantically searched the open-plan office. Like curious prairie dogs, heads throughout the room poked up from behind their light blue walls, but after realizing Mencken was no one of importance, they retreated back into their holes.

Mencken's eyes scanned the outskirts of the room. The walls were lined with glass rooms. Most seemed to be private offices, small spaces with a single desk or two.

Finally, he found the room he needed – a large conference room filled with people.

Mencken strode across the room, pushed the door open, and charged into the midst of the meeting. Winchell was sitting at the head of a long brown table, with four reporters crowded onto either side. They were all dressed in business-casual attire. They were mixed in ages, genders, and races, but they all had the stressed, pasty look of writers who'd spent too much time inside under deadlines. Mencken had met some of them. These were the division chiefs for the Star.

Sam, who was at the far end of the table from Winchell, looked up, smiled, and said, "Hey, Mencken. Surprised to see you here."

"Shut up, Sam," Mencken barked. "Richard, I need to talk with you. Right now."

"You look like shit, Mencken," Winchell replied. "Everyone," he said to the room. "This is Mencken Cassie. Brings us great stuff, but isn't quite ready for a desk yet."

"Loved the stuff on the sex-trafficking bust you sent us," said a gray-haired, heavyset man in a white button-down with rolled up sleeves. "Three sites busted at once. An interview with the property owner. That was good work. Wish I could get the cops to listen to me like that."

"Richard," Mencken pleaded, holding back tears. "Please. Please. I need to talk to you."

"Shoot kid," Winchell said. "If it's a story it's going to end up in this room anyway."

"I, um. I." Mencken could feel tears building behind his eyes. The imagined sound of the Cleveland child returned, rattling softly in the back of his mind. "I. I, um." He took deep breaths, trying to calm himself.

"Spit it out kid," Winchell demanded. "Shit or get off the pot."

Tears trickled from his eyes. "There all, um. There all connected. Everything. It's. It's all connected."

Winchell sat forward. "What are talking about?"

Mencken wiped his eyes with the back of his hand. "The hit in the park. The murder of Angela Dickson. The fires at the two bars. The kidnapping four months ago. The hit-and-run on Councilman Jackman's son at Easter. The death of that priest over in Sandtown last year. And the. And the-" Mencken stumbled, struggling to find words. Tears flowed fresh again. He closed his eyes and saw Alexander on the floor. He saw the wound in Tamara Cleveland's neck. He saw the child in her lap. A barrier broke inside of him. Water streamed from his eyes, leaving streaks on his cheeks. "And the Clevelands. And the. The Clevelands. They're all connected."

"I heard you were there," Sam said. "They told us you were the first on the scene? You doing okay?"

Rage filled Mencken's chest. Pounding on the table with both hands, he screamed, "Shut the fuck up, Sam! Just shut up! I'm trying to tell you. I'm trying to tell you, they're all the same person. Every hit. They were all done by the same killer. He's like a hitman. But he's not a hitman. He's more a, a, a cleaner, of sorts. He does things. He does things for the Cabal. And he killed the Clevelands. Last night. He stabbed their baby." The rage was replaced again by sorrow and tears. "He stabbed their baby. Who. Who stabs a baby? Who does that?"

"Slow down, kid," Winchell said in a soothing tone. "Just slow down." He rubbed his forehead and looked at the ceiling. Then he looked back to Mencken. "Listen kid, when was the last time you slept?"

"Goddamn it!" Mencken raged again. "I don't need sleep. I don't. I just. I just need to catch him. I need him gone. So. So I can write it. I can put it all together. I can do it. I'll outline everything." Mencken's head and lungs began to hurt. He was suddenly aware of how dry his mouth was. He needed a drink of something. His lips and tongue burned. "I just need you to run it, Richard. I need you to promise to run it. Please. Please. I need you to promise." Words were becoming difficult. The room rocked making Mencken felt like he was on a ship. He couldn't catch his breath. "Please," he gasped. "Please, just. Just promise to run it. Just." Everyone was staring at him. His legs were suddenly weak. He braced himself on the table. "I just. He can't hide anymore, Richard. He can't."

Sam caught him mid-fall, almost collapsing under Mencken's weight. He held Mencken up, saying softly over and over, "It's going to be okay. It'll be okay. It's going to be alright."

Winchell was standing. Many in the room had come to their feet when Mencken fell. "It's going to be alright," Winchell said.

"He stabbed the baby," Mencken whispered, bracing himself on Sam and the table. "He put the baby in his mother's lap, and then he stabbed them both in the neck. While his mom held him. He just stabbed him. They died together. Bleeding out."

"Jesus," Winchell said.

Sam rubbed Mencken's back. "Let's go get you cleaned up," he said. "Marge will get you some coffee. We'll splash some water in your face. Then you can tell us all about it."

Sam led Mencken to a bathroom. Mencken didn't recognize himself in the mirror. His eyes carried heavy bags. His mustache and goatee had begun to clot together from tears, vomit, and snot. There was bruising around his neck and a fresh cut on his cheek. He splashed water in his face. It ran down his mustache and filled his nose. Holding himself up with both hands on the sink in front of him, he closed his eyes. He felt like he might pass out. Behind his lids, he saw the expression on the Cleveland baby's face again. Vomit rose in his throat and the room began to spin. He gripped both sides of the sink to keep from falling over. Breathing deeply, he tried to force calm, to regain control. After a few minutes, he began to feel stronger. He took another look at himself. He was still there, behind the exhaustion.

A smiling face appeared behind him in the mirror. "You're Goddamn Mencken Cassie," Sam said, putting his hands on Mencken's shoulders. "Pull yourself together. You've got a story to tell. Because you're goddamn Mencken Cassie."

"I'm goddamn Mencken Cassie," Mencken repeated. His body tingled with each word. "I'm goddamn Mencken Cassie."

Sam rubbed his shoulders. "You're goddamn Mencken Cassie," he said with pride. "And you've got a story to tell."

Mencken sighed. "Thank you, Sam," he said.

Sam clapped him on the back. "Come on," he said. "Let's get back in there."

When Sam and Mencken returned to the conference room, there were only two people left at the table. Winchell stood and introduced the man sitting next to his left. "Mencken Cassie, this is Don Angelus. Don is working the Cleveland story for us."

Don offered his hand to Mencken and the two men shook. "I know your work," Don said. "I've been looking forward to putting a face with a byline."

"Thanks," Mencken said quietly. He wished he could return the compliment. The truth was, he didn't recognize the name. He couldn't place anything the man had written. Mencken took the seat to Winchell's left. Sam took the next chair.

"Alright," Winchell said. "Start from the beginning. You said the word 'Cabal.'" He put air quotes around the title as if it were a ridiculous notion.

Mencken looked at his hands. They were folded on the table. His eye lids were heavy and his head ached. A voice in his gut demanded he remain silent. It screamed that he was about to give up his Pulitzer to no-name Don, but Mencken was too tired to fight anymore. He couldn't muster the will to hold things close to his chest. He knew he needed help.

"I first noticed them when the casino went up," Mencken started. He kept his eyes focused on his hands during the explaining. He was nervous that if he looked up, he'd see the other three men laughing at him. He was afraid they'd call him crazy.

Mencken explained the patterns he'd begun to notice. The strategic increase and then sharp decrease in crime. The way the three development companies bought low, rebuilt, and then sold high once the crime had cooled. He talked about cops and criminals with nice houses and cars in the suburbs. He shared about council people taking bribes and kickbacks for paving the way for development. He confessed to harassing members of the Cabal in order to get a response, to going to Agamemnon's house, and then this morning to Hammerjam's office.

Then finally, he came to the enforcer. "And so," Mencken said softly. "When they run into a problem they can't overcome in the normal way, they call out their hitman. And he takes care of it. Like with Alexander Cleveland. He was going after the development companies for misappropriation of funds. Well, at least I thought he was. I had a source in his office who said he was. But then," Mencken remembered what Hammerjam had said about he and Cleveland being friends. "I don't know. I just don't know." He rubbed his right eye with his palm. "A source told me he was. And they couldn't make him stop. So last they killed him. They killed him and his family."

"I believe you," Sam said.

"Shut up, Sam," Winchell barked. He was leaning back in his chair with his arms crossed. "The problem is, kid. You don't have any proof. It's a good theory, but you've got nothing concrete. Do you even know who this hitman is?"

Mencken took his phone out and slid it to Winchell. "Open my Twitter account," he said.

Winchell slid the phone back. "Please. Do I look like a twelve-year-old girl to you? I don't know how to use that."

Sam picked up the phone, passed it to Mencken to unlock, then took it back. He scrolled around for around for minute or two. "The guy's been sending him notes, Dick. He's been taunting him."

"Gimmie that," Winchell said. He looked through the Twitter feed too. "It's too generic. This doesn't prove anything. Someone might even accuse you of making this all up yourself."

"I know," Mencken said. "But I didn't. It's real."

Winchell sat forward and rubbed his temples with his middle fingers. "I believe you," he said, shaking his head. "Jesus. I believe you. But you've got more work to do. You can't play conjecture with this one. You've got to have cold, hard, facts. No online, blogging, guess-here, insinuation-there bullshit. You've got to do this old-school. You get the proof. Then we go to print."

Mencken nodded.

"You got a suspect? Or a lead?"

"Yeah," Mencken said. "I know who it is."

"Great. Tail his ass. Keep on him. He'll do something stupid. You got anything to add," Winchell asked no-byline Don.

"Yeah," Don said. "Stop fucking with them until you finish the story. This is serious shit. They'll kill. And if they kill you then we've got no story. So lay low."

"Agreed," Winchell said, smacking the table. "They already know you're coming. You've got to keep a low profile now. Make them think the Clevelands scared the shit out of you. No more tweeting. No more public confrontations. Put it all in the work. Got it?"

"Yes, sir," Mencken said.

"Okay," Winchell said, standing. "Good. Now, go home. Take a nap. Eat something. Take a damn shower. Then write some shit down. You'll feel better."

"Thank you," Mencken said. Then he stood and walked toward the door.

CHAPTER SEVENTEEN

Suspecting Chris and Jose were early risers, Mencken began staking out Imani's a little before five in the morning – a good five hours before his usual appearance at the shop. The duo emerged thirty minutes later. They shot from the door and continued at a quick pace down the empty sidewalk like men on a mission. Mencken looked at his motorcycle and wondered what the best way to follow them was. He decided that as long as they were on foot, he would be on foot too.

The first stage of Chris and Jose's energetic morning walk lasted six hours. Leaving Imani's, they traveled north on President Street to Pleasant, where they crossed under Interstate 83 and made their way to Franklin. They followed Franklin to Pennsylvania Avenue, where they took Liberty Heights. From there, they went north to Forest Park, looping back south until they were on the northwest side of Leakin Park.

It was a journey Mencken was painfully unprepared for. While Chris and Jose were still spry, Mencken was dragging his feet. He longed for a place to sit and relax. His feet ached and his jeans were beginning to rub his thighs raw. A few times on the journey, Mencken considered calling out to the pair ahead and begging them to slow down. Every shop they passed brought with it the temptation to pull up and try to find the duo later, but Mencken never gave into the temptation. Discovering them in the midst of a nefarious deed was too important. His desire to catch them drove him forward, one agonizing step at a time.

At nine o'clock, Jose and Chris turned back east, following Windsor Mill road through the middle of Leakin Park. Trailing the two travelers through the overgrown woods was difficult. Rather than sticking to the roads as they had been for most of the morning, the pair took a semi-scenic route, trudging through rougher, uncut terrain. Realizing shuffling through the underbrush was a noisy endeavor, Mencken allowed more distance between himself and his quarry.

They emerged from the woods somewhere in the Poplar Grove neighborhood. Quickly Mencken found himself in a warehouse district he had never seen. He was stunned, stumbling through large brick box-like buildings. Until today, he thought he'd covered every inch of the city. Now, he wondered how many hidden corners there were that he'd never seen. While finding new places in a beloved city might be exciting for some, for Mencken it was unsettling. It meant there were things happening, potential stories of which he was unaware. He made a mental note that he would need to explore this area more on his own when all of this was over.

At Baltimore Street, the pair cut southeast to Pratt. Mencken's confidence began to return. He'd walked Pratt a thousand times. They passed the Ravens' Stadium and Camden Yards. They strolled through the Inner Harbor, passed the concert arena, and stopped back to the foot of interstate 83.

Once they reached the high-trafficked streets of Downtown and Mencken saw people talking and laughing, people making phone calls and reading newspapers,

Mencken realized how strange the walk had been. Chris and Jose hadn't stopped to speak with anyone. They weren't running an errand or heading to a specific destination. They hadn't picked anything up, dropped anything off, or stalked anyone. At the same time, their walk wasn't exercise. They weren't keeping a consistent pace or pushing themselves. Occasionally, especially downtown, they slowed to a stroll. Other times, in empty spaces mostly, they almost jogged. At all times, the two were hyper-vigilant, looking down every alley and peering down every side street, observing every sound and every movement. It was almost as if they were searching for something. As if the entire city were a haystack, and they were looking for a needle.

At the end of President Street, they came to a twelve-story parking garage intended for patrons of the waterfront Marriot. Mencken watched Chris and Jose enter through the car entrance. They proceeded up the ramps, unfazed by the incline. Mencken's legs screamed in protest at the thought of pursuing the would-be-killers up the steep ramps.

Mencken stopped, bent over, and rubbed his calves and thighs. His jeans were soaked with sweat. His feet had moved from pain into a raw numbness. This isn't at all how he had thought the day would go. He had expected Chris and Jose to lounge somewhere until the hitman and his protégé got a call from whomever gave them orders. Then they would snap into action, and Mencken would be there to catch them in the act. He had not foreseen an incredibly boring tour of the city.

He looked at the ramp. He didn't think he was capable of tackling the inclines. He'd probably fall dead of exhaustion and dehydration somewhere on the second floor. His gut told him they were going to the roof. They seemed to be on the lookout for something. The roof made sense. Once they had cleared the first floor, Mencken took the elevator up. He beat them to the top.

Stepping off the elevator, he searched for somewhere to hide. The lot was littered with cars, but most were small and isolated. There was a white pickup truck parked in a corner. It appeared to be the only vehicle big enough to give Mencken cover. He lay on his stomach and scooted underneath it. From his resting place, he could see almost the entire top floor. It was perfect.

It felt good to lie down, even if it was on the hard surface of a parking lot under a truck. His legs and feet sighed with relief. His mouth and throat were parched. His clothes clung to his skin. He wanted nothing more than to go home and sleep.

A car emerged from the ramp. It was a beat up, brown, BMW from the 80's. It parked across from Mencken's position. He couldn't have placed it better in his line of sight if he'd been directing traffic. To his surprise, Imani stepped from the driver's seat. She retrieved a brown picnic basket from the trunk, took it to the hood of the car, and sat down, watching the city beneath her.

Moments later Chris and Jose emerged from the ramp. Jose laughed and ran to her. Mencken grumbled to himself, confused as to how the boy still had the energy to run. The three ate and chatted on the hood of the car, watching the city below.

Mencken didn't like it. Imani didn't fit into his image of the cold, heartless, lone hitman doing the bidding of the Cabal for the money and the rush of the kill. He wasn't prepared for Chris: a homeless vagrant, living in the basement of a bar, building a family with a woman Mencken respected, taking picnic lunch breaks at the top of parking garages.

Mencken studied the car, wondering if it was the same one on the night he saved Anita Dickson. Was it the same as the one outside the Cleveland's house? He fought to recall the other images.

Maybe.

Maybe was the best he could do. He needed to be

careful not to rewrite history to support the narrative he was building.

Mencken wished he could hear them. He tried to read their lips, but all he saw was gibberish. He watched the trio with curiosity, wondering what he had missed about Imani, wondering how much about him she had shared with them. She didn't seem like the type of woman who would be attracted to a serial killer. Maybe she didn't know? But how could the night of chaos in her bar have happened if she didn't know? She had to know. She was a part of it. There was no other explanation.

Mencken slid his arms sideways, struggling to retrieve his phone from his pocket. Twice, his elbow became wedged between the exhaust pipe and his chest. Finally, he managed to maneuver the phone where he could see the screen. It occurred to him that he hadn't looked at his phone all day. His Twitter message box was overflowing with tips, questions, and comments. His email had grown exponentially. Skimming the senders, he found one from Winchell requesting an update on his progress. Mencken wrote back, "Chasing the lead. I think I have him. Waiting for him to act."

Mencken looked to the three again. They were laughing together. Jose and Imani sat on the hood of the car while Chris stood to Imani's left. He had half a ham sandwich in his hand. "They're not going anywhere," Mencken told himself. His eyelids were heavy. They longed close. He watched Jose pop open a can of soda. "I can take a few minutes." Mencken allowed his eyes to shut, telling himself he'd only sleep for five minutes or so.

"Hey, you!" the voice yelled. Something was poking Mencken in the side. Trying to sit up, he whacked his head on the metal undercarriage of the truck.

"Get out from under my truck," a male voice with a deep southern twang demanded. Mencken tried to clear his head. It was his aching in his legs that reminded him of where he was.

"Come on now," the voice said again. "I'm fixin' to pull out. I've got somewhere to be." A stick poked Mencken in the side again.

"Alright. Alright," he said. "I'm coming out." Gingerly, he slid out from beneath the truck. Except for the heavyset man in khakis and a blue sports coat standing in front of Mencken, the parking lot was empty. He'd lost them.

"Hey, buddy," the heavy man said. "That's just not a good place to sleep. I could have killed you. If I hadn't of just happen to check my back tire, I might have run right over you."

"What time is it?" Mencken said, trying to clear his head.

"It's five-thirty. I'm on my way to dinner. Seriously, I could have killed you."

"Yeah, yeah," Mencken said, walking away. "Sorry. Have a nice night."

Every step was agony. It took him forty-five minutes to walk the half-mile back to his apartment. Once upstairs, he downed four glasses of water, standing over the sink and refilling each one. He decided that tomorrow, he didn't care if they were on foot; he would take his motorcycle.

Around seven, his cell lit up with Twitter messages. A four-alarm fire at the corner of Bank and Wolf. It felt good to be back into his routine. He grabbed his backpack and headed down the stairs to his bike. He was at the blaze in seconds. Three fire trucks doused three burning rowhomes with powerful streams of water. A crowd had gathered to watch the bout between the sworn enemies, firefighter and fire.

Mencken parked his motorcycle on the sidewalk a block down and walked over. Jostling for position, moving to the front of the mob like someone with authority, Mencken made it all the way to the wooden barrier the police had thrown together. Pulling out his cell, he took a video of the event and immediately posted it to Twitter. It seemed the firemen had given up on saving the three burning houses and were instead trying to contain the blaze.

Mencken scanned the crowd, hoping to find someone who might be able to give him some comment or insight into how the fire started. The only person who stood out was a tiny man standing across from Mencken, at the front of the crowd. The man couldn't have been more than four feet tall. He was perfectly proportioned, just small, and oddly dressed. The tiny man wore a full tuxedo with tails, a black cummerbund, a bow tie, and a monocle. The only other person Mencken had ever seen wear a monocle was Natty Boh, the mascot of National Bohemian beer.

Even more than the man's size and clothes, what stuck out was his excitement. Watching the fire, the small man bounced up and down and clapped his hands with glee. Like a child about to see his first movie, his excitement was palpable.

Mencken thought such enthusiasm about a disaster was odd. He decided that this was the man he needed to talk to about what was going on. Surely, this man with all his exuberance would know what had happened. He'd at least have a story to tell. Mencken moved to walk in the man's direction.

"What'cha doing?" a young voice came from Mencken's left. He turned and looked down. Jose was standing there next to him, watching the fire.

"Yeah," a female voice said from his right. "What'cha doing?" Mencken looked to see Agnew on his other side.

"Jose. Agnew," Mencken said. "Aren't you missing two?"

"Rothman doesn't come out for stuff like this," Jose said.

"Why's that?" Mencken asked, keeping his eyes on the small man. The man was bouncing from one foot to the other now in a dance of joy.

"Feels it's beneath him," Agnew said.

There was a loud bang from the fire as a fourth rowhome started to burn. Mencken's attention was drawn away for a moment. It was hard not to be entranced by the fire. The dance of the flames called to Mencken. Gazing at the fourth home, watching it burn, Mencken asked, "Where's your boy Chris?"

"He's around," Jose said, not taking his eyes off the fire.

"What did you do today?" Mencken asked.

"Patrolled," Jose answered.

"For monsters?" Mencken said, with a belittling tone.

"Yep," Jose said. "Every day's the same."

Mencken looked over at the small man again. The man was playing with his monocle, moving toward and away from his eye, as if he were trying to focus it on the fire. Then Mencken noticed a figure behind the man. Was it Chris? It was difficult to tell.

Agnew stepped into his line of view. "What did you do today?"

Realizing he was being diverted, Menken pushed passed her, moving toward Chris and the small man. The small man didn't seem to be aware of Chris' presence. Mencken tried to wade through the crowd, but more people were coming to the barricade to watch the firefighters do battle.

Jose grabbed Mencken by the arm. His grip was surprisingly strong. "How are the stories coming?" he said. "Imani said you had something new? Something big?"

"Get off me," he said, pushing the teen's hand off his sleeve. Then looking back up, he searched the crowd for the small man or Chris. Both had disappeared. Mencken looked back to his left. Jose and Agnew were gone too. "Son of a bitch," Mencken yelled. A day of pursuit and nothing to show for it.

CHAPTER EIGHTEEN

Mencken was proud of himself. Today, he'd come prepared. His backpack was full of water and snacks, he was in comfortable pants he knew wouldn't chafe, and best of all, he was on his bike. Already it had been far superior to trying to keep up with these crazy marathon speed-walkers. Unfortunately, it meant Mencken couldn't have constant eyes on Chris and Jose, as he was having to circle them to keep from being seen.

Jose and Chris had started off the morning by going north, up Wolfe Street. After passing Hopkins Hospital, the pair took a right on Gay Street and followed it all the way to the Overlea Diner. Once again, Imani meet them in the parking lot with lunch. The ride had been uneventful for Mencken. He tried to stay two blocks behind the pair at all times, turning right or left every five minutes to create more distance between them.

Rather than napping under a truck, during lunch Mencken took up residence at the Pizza Hut across the street. He watched the trio eat together from the restaurant's window. While this day was far more favorable than the one before, Mencken was hoped he could catch Chris in something soon. He was ready to be back on the beat, hitting the streets, covering the ins and outs of the city. It was only his second day on the stakeout and he was already bored. He thought trailing a hitman would be more entertaining.

There was more wandering after lunch. Chris and Jose headed east on Hamilton Avenue until they hit Perring Parkway. Then they turned south toward Morgan State University. Just as the day before, the pair changed pace on occasion, but was ever vigilant, looking down every street, stopping at every alley.

At 33rd Street something changed. Mencken was two blocks back when Chris stopped moving. It was the first time in two days when Mencken had seen the pair come to a complete halt. Mencken pulled closer, wanting a better look. He watched Chris take something out of his pocket. Maybe a flip phone? Jose scanned the street in both directions. He seemed to be standing guard on heightened alert.

Mencken's heart raced. If Chris was getting a call, maybe the wandering was about to end? Maybe he was about to jump into action? Mencken wondered who the hit was on. He wanted to get closer, to get a better look at what was going on, maybe even get close enough to hear what Chris was saying, but he knew they would hear his motorcycle approaching. Chris put the phone back in his pocket and the duo broke into a small jog. Mencken's heart skipped. This was it, the moment he'd been waiting for. He was sure of it. He'd catch them in the act and bring this whole ring crashing down.

At the corner of 33rd and Old York Road, a truck appeared. It was a beat-up, gray, Toyota from the 80's. Chris and Jose jumped into the bed. As the truck took a left to the south, Mencken strained to see the driver. He thought it was Agnew, but it was difficult to tell. Suddenly, it occurred to him that he could no longer stay so far behind and still keep up. Revving his engine, he maneuvered his bike between cars in the left and right lane, racing to catch the trio.

He turned left and spotted the truck seven cars ahead of him. Jose and Chris were chatting in the bed. It didn't appear they had noticed him. He slowed his pace again, hoping to remain concealed. The pickup continued south on Greenmount. Mencken couldn't help but try and hypothesize about where they were headed. Maybe this was an errand for Agamemnon? Mencken wasn't sure which gang was currently in charge in these neighborhoods. Or maybe they were headed back toward City Hall? Would this be another hit on a do-gooder like Anita Dixon? Would they blow up more property? Would they kill another prosecutor like Alexander Cleveland? Mencken was torn. Part of him hoped they were simply headed home, and that no one would be hurt. Part of him hoped a huge story was about to unfold, something that would be enough to prove Chris was the hitman, something that might land him on the front page again. He could taste the Pulitzer.

The truck took a left down a small side street. Mencken slowed not wanting to bump into them on accident. He pulled up at the corner and glanced down the street. The gray pickup was driving slowly down Biddle Street. Chris and Jose were standing in the bed, searching for something, one looking left and the other looking right. Mencken followed, hanging a few blocks behind, doing his best to remain inconspicuous.

The street was a mix of occupied and abandoned rowhomes, with an occasional empty lot where a rundown house had been demolished and the rubble carted away. The pickup slowed and pulled into a parking spot on the street. A block ahead, Mencken saw a small group of tall men. They were strong, bald, and wore matching loose-fitting clothes. The common dress suggested they were part of some strange gang, but Mencken had no clue which one. If they saw the pickup truck, they didn't let on. Rather, they seemed to be laughing about something.

Mencken watched as Chris and Jose crouched in the bed of the truck and conferred. Then, to Mencken's surprise, Jose hopped out of the bed onto the sidewalk. Chris disappeared into the bed. Agnew pulled out of the parking spot and turned right, down the nearest alley. Alone, Jose began walking toward the group of men. Mencken felt an odd mix of fear and curiosity. Who was this kid who walked toward a group of thugs with no fear?

Mencken edged his bike forward to get a better look. As Jose approached the group, Mencken began to feel real terror on Jose's behalf. It was clear that those giant men could rip a small kid like Jose to shreds. Mencken parked his bike. He thought about calling out, getting Jose's attention, trying to insert himself into the situation before something terrible happened. He wondered where Chris and Agnew had gone. How could Chris leave his sidekick out here alone to get a beating? Mencken walked briskly toward Jose, still trying to maintain his cover, but closing the gap in case he needed to step in and save the young teen.

To Mencken's shock, fifteen yards before Jose reached the gang, the teen called out. Mencken couldn't tell what he said, but it seemed to strike fear into the hearts of the three thugs. They looked at each other, looked at Jose, and ran in the opposite direction. Jose gave chase. Mencken watched with confusion. None of this made any sense to him. It struck him that he should be running as well if he wanted to record whatever this bizarre story might turn out to be.

The three thugs took a turn to the left into an empty lot between two abandoned homes. Jose was quick on their heels. As Mencken approached the lot, he was forced to slow his pace. He didn't know what he would find on the other side. Pressing his back against the corner of the rowhome next to the empty lot, he waited and listened. There were no sounds of struggle, no indications that some sort of fight was happening. There was nothing.

"You dumbass," Mencken said to himself. "You've probably lost them." Mencken hadn't considered that this empty lot connected two streets. He'd assumed it was a dead end, but that might not have been the case. It's possible the thugs had taken a second left and just kept running.

Mencken took a breath and then peered around the corner. There were no thugs. There was no fight. There was simply the gray pickup blocking an exit out of the lot. Agnew and Chris were securing a gray tarp over the top of the truck bed. Jose was sitting in the middle seat of the truck. A brisk wind whipped through the open lot. It tore the tarp from Agnew's hands, revealing the contents of the bed. Mencken stumbled back at the site of the three tugs, their limbs twisted, their faces contorted, laying lifeless in the back of the pickup. Agnew caught the tarp and tugged it back over the truck bed.

Knowing the trio was getting ready to leave with Mencken's evidence in the bed of the truck, Mencken turned and sprinted toward his bike. Arriving at it, he gunned the motor and pulled out of his spot. Roaring down the street, concerned less about secrecy and more about missing his chance to catch them, Mencken whipped his bike to the left, into the abandoned lot, but the truck was gone. He passed through to the street on the other side. Frantically looking left and right, he couldn't decide which way to go. "Son of a bitch," he yelled. He'd lost them again.

CHAPTER NINETEEN

Mencken sat at the red light, two blocks behind Chris and Jose. His eyes were intensely focused, watching their every move. He studied how Chris walked, how he gave Jose a few words of direction every block or so. After trailing them for three days, Mencken had come to understand their teacher/student relationship on a deeper level. Chris was constantly sharing insight with Jose. Mencken imaged these small conversations to be important notes in the life of a hitman. Maybe how best to enter a rowhome undetected, or how to snap a man's neck in a single move, or how to dispose of three gangbanger bodies. It was impossible for Mencken to know what was really being said. What he could see was Jose's response to everything Chris said. Chris would whisper something and Jose would nod in appreciation.

Menken's vigor for the chase had been restored last night. Rosie had filled in some holes on his wall. She had shared two facts that had particularly stirred Mencken's blood. First, on the night Mencken had seen Chris' cohort in chaos at Imani's, the night Melody had disappeared, there had been a large gang fight at the mouth of Druid Hill Park. A group loyal to Agamemnon had faced off with what had been described by onlookers as "a gang of hairless, pale, weightlifters." A third party had interceded and ended the fight before the police had arrived. Witnesses said the third party had loaded many of the bodies into the back of a gray pickup truck. Hours later there had been a massive fire at a dock on the southwest side of town. Rosie explained they were still examining the remnants of the blaze for human remains.

She also explained that a similar fire had sparked up in an empty house in Dundalk on the east side of the city yesterday afternoon. A neighbor said she saw three people unloading bodies from a pickup truck and taking them into the house just before it caught fire. The house had completely burned to the ground.

Upon hearing these facts, Mencken was convinced of three things. First, there was a gang war going on with a new set of players, probably from out of town. The pale body builders were facing off with the Cabal. Second, Chris was the Cabal hitman, and he was patrolling the streets looking for rival gang members. Finally, Mencken was going to be the man who revealed this horrible killer to the world, and in turn, shined light on the Cabal, revealing how it was destroying his city for money.

Chris and Jose had stopped again. Mencken knew he needed to get closer. He wasn't going to lose them this time. Just as before, Chris put the flip phone up to his ear while Jose stood guard. Mencken sped up, weaving through the afternoon traffic on Charles, desperate to close the gap between himself and his prey before they made a break for it. He knew on foot they could lose him if they cut blocks by running through alleys. He had to stay on their heels.

Mencken glanced up as he slid between two cars. He saw Chris put the phone in his pocket, turn to Jose, and explain something. They must have received a tip. The duo shot from their position to the right, down North Avenue. As Mencken neared the corner, he slowed and pulled onto the sidewalk. Glancing around the corner, he saw the two wanderers running fast.

The wide sidewalks of North Avenue were empty, giving Chris and Jose the ability to sprint unhindered, but the street was filled with routine traffic, making it difficult for Mencken to keep up. The light in front of him turned red, forcing him to wait. "Son of a bitch," Mencken exclaimed as Chris and Jose darted across the median, crossing to the other side of the four-lane street. They sprinted passed a large empty parking lot, a nondescript building built in the 80's, and a large white church with giant oak doors. They hung a left at the corner of the church and they were gone.

"Not again," Mencken growled under his breath. He eased his bike forward to the stop line and watched for a break in the traffic. A yellow Oldsmobile paused to turn left. Mencken leapt on the chance. Gunning the motor, he sped through the light with reckless abandon. There was a blare of horns and a screeching of tires, metal crushed against rubber as cars collided, but Mencken soared through without a scratch.

Again, he slowed at the corner. His eyes went wide and his stomach churned. The pickup was back, pulled against the side of the road. There were large black puddles in the street. Jose sat, learning against the gray stone wall of the church. His face, hands, and shirt were splattered with the black substance. He was removing fingerless gloves and cleaning the black goop from them.

Mencken was filled with a mix of sorrow and elation at the sight of Chris and Agnew loading four large, white, bodies into the bed of the truck. Mencken took his cell phone out and snapped pictures, capturing Chris and Agnew heaving the lifeless bodies over the side of the vehicle.

Chris took the final body beneath the arms. Agnew took its legs. They swung it back and forth and then, using all their might, tossed it into the pickup. Mencken texted a video to Rosie with the simple message. "Corner of Saint Paul and North Ave. I got them. In pursuit." Seconds later his phone rang.

At each corner, Mencken gave Rosie an update on the pickup's location. Three cop cars intercepted the truck at the corner of Calvert and 30th streets. The blue-and-whites formed a triangle around the vehicle, boxing it into the intersection. Red and blue lights filled the beautiful street, illuminating the three-story rowhomes. The houses on the block were grand, complete with covered porches and large, green, bay windows on the second floor. Mencken pulled over onto the sidewalk and began recording the scene with his cell phone.

Six uniformed cops sprang from their cars and took cover behind car doors and trunks, their weapons extended toward the pickup. Multiple voices screamed for the occupants of the truck to exit their vehicle with their hands up. More cars screeched to a halt, joining the blockade. Some were standard blue and white police cars with their lights flashing, others were ordinary-looking Fords.

Detective Rosario Jimenez stepped from the passenger seat of one of the unmarked cars. Drawing her weapon, she moved toward the pickup truck. "Get out of the car with your hands in the air," she screamed. The rest of the police automatically submitted to her lead. Mencken was entranced by her stoic focus. She wore a gray pantsuit with a purple blouse. "Someday," he whispered to himself with regret.

The doors of the pickup truck pushed open. The officers held their breath, bracing for the worst. Chris, Agnew, and Jose stepped from the car with their hands up. Mencken noticed Agnew's leg was still bothering her by the way she favored her right leg as she climbed from the cab.

"Lay down on the ground, with your hands behind your head," Rosie screamed. "Right now!"

Chris smiled, but not with victory or pride. It was a smile of apology. "Don't shoot," he yelled, edging toward the bed of the truck.

"Stop right there," Rosie screamed back. "Don't make us kill you."

"Don't shoot," Chris yelled, still moving slowly to the bed of the truck. His hands held high in surrender. "Don't shoot."

"Get down on the ground," Rosie screamed, her voice cracking with rage.

Mencken noticed a glint of sunlight bounce off of Chris' right hand. He was holding something silver and small. Mencken wanted to scream out to Rosie, but before he could, Chris made his move.

Chris looked down at the ground and swallowed. Looking up again he said, "Now." In one smooth motion, he flicked up the silver lighter igniting a small flame, dropped it into the bed of the truck, and fell to the ground. In less than seconds, the back of the pickup erupted in flames. The wave of power from the blast forced everyone watching to look away. In response, guns unloaded.

"Hold your fire," Rosie screamed. "Hold your fire." More voices echoed her command. A cloud of black smoke enveloped the truck. The officers waited with jaws clenched to see what was left of the truck and its crew.

When the chaos had stopped, the truck was riddled with holes and filled with broken glass. The fire in the bed continued to blaze sending an unending stream of black smoke into the air. Chris and Agnew lay on the ground next to one another, their fingers interlaced behind their heads, but Jose was gone.

CHAPTER TWENTY

Mencken looked at himself in the small bathroom mirror. There was still bruising around his neck. Both his eyes were bloodshot. He looked like hell. "Occupied," he called as someone tried the door knob.

"It's me," Rosie said from the other side of the door. "Let's go."

The pair walked quickly from the bathroom down the hall, hoping no one would notice Mencken entering the observation room. The small space had two chairs and a desk with some rudimentary recording equipment on it. Through the glass in front of them, Mencken and Rosie watched Frank Benny review the notes Rosie had given him minutes before. Frank was a short overweight cop in his forties. His suit was rumbled and there was a coffee stain on his yellow tie.

"It should be me in there," Rosie grumbled.

"Yep," Mencken said. The minute they had stepped into the station, the senior detective had ripped the case from Rosie and demanded a full briefing. Mencken was sure Detective Benny was acting under the influence of the Cabal, but Rosie assured him that Frank was just a lazy asshole who used his seniority to poach cases.

"Goddamn, lazy-ass, redneck hick," Rosie said. "Get your own goddamn case."

"Yep," Mencken said again. In truth, he wasn't too broken up about it. Rosie had only agreed to sneak him in to watch because she was pissed she wasn't the one who'd get to question Chris. Before the case was stolen from her, she was demanding Mencken go home, telling him she'd call him later.

Chris sat in the metal chair across from Frank, his back straight and eyes his focused forward. His hands rested, motionlessly on the table he was handcuffed to.

"So what do you think?" Mencken asked. "You think Frank can get a confession out of him?"

"No way in hell," she said.

Rosie took off her blazer, folded it gently, laid it on a chair, and took a seat. She rolled up her sleeves revealing the tattoo on her forearm of an eagle standing on a globe with an anchor through it. The sight of it always made Mencken wonder where else she had tattoos. He sighed and took the chair next to her.

Detective Benny closed the manila folder he'd been flipping through and laid it on the table in front of Chris. Benny waited to see if the suspect would look down at it. He didn't.

"For your information and for the record, I will be recording this," Detective Benny said, turning on the small video recorder mounted to the table by his left hand. "Do you understand?"

"Yes?" Chris said.

Mencken could tell Benny was frustrated by the suspect's reply. The questioning tone wouldn't hold up in court. Mencken smiled. At a minimum, this was going to be entertaining.

"Was that a question?" Frank asked, dismissively.

"Yes."

"What don't you understand?"

"Right now?"

"Yes. Right now. What don't you understand right now?"

"Why do I have to be in handcuffs?" Chris asked.

"Alright, wise ass," Detective Benny said, leaning back in his chair and crossing his arms. "Let's try this again. Once more, do you understand that this is being recorded? It really doesn't matter, but for the sake of the rest of this conversation, do you understand?"

"No?"

"Are you trying to make this difficult?" Benny said.

"Not at all, Officer," Chris said.

"Detective," Benny said.

"I'm not a detective. Not in any official capacity, although I do enjoy a good puzzle."

"I meant that I am a detective, not an officer."

"I thought all detectives had to be officers?"

"I mean, I am an officer, and I'm a detective. My title is Detective."

Rosie laughed and shook her head. She was enjoying watching Benny get tied in knots.

"How do you keep them straight?" Chris asked.

"Keep what straight?" Benny said.

"Being an officer and a detective."

"They're the same thing."

"Then why do they have different names?" Chris seemed genuinely confused, but Mencken knew better.

"Not all officers are detectives but all detectives are officers."

"Oh. Like not all cars are trucks, but all trucks are cars."

"No. Not like that at all."

"Like a mule is half horse and half donkey, but a pony has no donkey but some mule?"

"That doesn't even make any sense," Frank said.

"Or like a bulldog can be American or British, but never French or Canadian," Chris said. "Because a French-Canadian bulldog also doesn't make sense."

"Enough," Detective Benny said with frustration.

Rosie laughed again, this time louder.

Detective Benny sat forward in his chair. "I'll continue," he said, "with the understanding that you have been read your rights, and that this conversation is being recorded. Ok?"

"I've answered both yes and no. I'm not sure what answer is appropriate," Chris said.

"I shouldn't have said 'ok'. Neither answer is appropriate, because it doesn't make a difference."

"If neither answer is appropriate, than how are you supposed to know if I understand my rights?"

Detective Benny grabbed the camera and turned it toward his face. "Let the record show that the suspect has been informed of his rights," he said plainly. Then he turned the camera back toward the suspect and asked, "Your name is Chris, correct?"

"What does my folder say?"

Benny leaned back in his chair again. "Your folder says Chris."

"Ok, good."

"Why is that good?"

"Because if it said something different, I would have to give you different answers."

"Ok, I'm not sure I understand that, but it doesn't matter. Chris is your name, correct?"

"It's what's on my folder," Chris said, pointing to the folder on the table. "Says it right there."

"Forget the folder. Stop looking at the folder. Just tell me your name."

"Chris."

"Chris what?"

"No. Not what."

"Not what?"

"Not what."

"I'm confused."

"It's okay. I would be too, if I had two jobs."

"Two jobs?"

"Officer and detective."

"Goddamn it," Detective Benny said, lurching forward and smacking the table with both hands.

"I don't know why you're bringing God into this," Chris said.

"Son of bitch," Detective Benny said, rocking back in his chair, shaking his head.

Chris looked into the camera and gave it a confused shrug.

Detective Benny sat forward and leaned in close to the suspect. "Let's try this again. This conversation will be recorded. Do you understand what I am saying to you?" Chris began to speak, but the detective plowed forward. "Now, I don't want to hear about anything but the recording of the conversation. I don't want to hear about your cuffs, or the temperature of the room, or French-Canadian bulldogs. I only want to hear that you understand that everything said in this room will be recorded. Do you need me to explain that fact in any more detail?"

"No," Chris said.

"Excellent. Now, please state your full first and last name." Benny smiled with confidence, believing he was in charge again in the room.

"Christian Gracanjo Junior."

"Gracanjo? Is that Spanish?"

"It's more like a title. Actually, I think it's a curse word. In Latin."

"What?"

"I know, right?"

"Can you explain your last statement please?"

"Sure. Legend says it's what the army across the Veil called the first one of us when we kicked their asses for the first time."

"Whose ass did you kick?"

"Oh, I wasn't there. That battle was in Rome. I've

never been to Rome. But it's where we got the name. We kicked their asses, and they screamed as we pushed them back into Midian, 'Gracanjo!' That's why I think it's a curse word. I can't imagine they had anything nice to say. I mean, screaming something like, 'Flowers and cotton candy' just doesn't make any sense. Rothman knows more about it all, you can ask him. What's your name?"

Benny stared at the suspect in utter confusion. "Detective Benny," he replied.

"Benny what?"

"Detective Benny is all you need."

"Strange first name. Brings the whole officer thing full circle though, Officer Detective Benny."

"No. My name isn't Detective. I just don't want to tell you my name."

"Why not?"

"Because it's not important, and it's none of your business."

"Oh. Don't say that. Your name's important."

Rosie laughed a third time.

"That's not what I meant," Benny said. "Yes. My name is important."

"Then what is it?"

"Fine. Frank. My first name is Frank. Now for God's sake," Detective Benny said shaking his head in disbelief. "Let's continue."

"If it is for his sake, then I am more than ready," Chris said.

"How do you know State's Attorney Alexander Cleveland?"

"I don't think I know State's Attorney Alexander Cleveland."

"Did you ever have any contact with him or his family?"

"Not that I can recall."

"Were you outside of his residence on the night of October 23rd?"

"Where is his residence?"

"Twenty-five fifteen Kentucky Avenue."

"Oh, I know where that is."

"Have you ever been there?"

"Sure. Plenty of times. It's right off Harford Road."

"So you do know State's Attorney Cleveland?"

"No."

"But you've been to his house."

"No."

"But you just said you know where it is."

"Yes."

"You've indicated you knew it was off Harford Road."

"Yes."

"So you've been there."

"Walked passed on patrol. Yes."

"On patrol?"

"Yes."

"Patrolling for what?"

"Work."

"What do you do?"

"I patrol."

"Is that your occupation?"

"I'm a monster hunter," Chris said with a grin.

"Have you ever been inside State's Attorney Cleveland's house?"

"No."

"Maybe you were hunting a monster in his living room?"

"No."

Detective Benny opened the folder on the table. Carefully, he removed three photos and placed them in front of the suspect. "Do you recognize this scene?"

Chris studied the photos with grim intensity. The first was of a man in a pool of blood, in a hallway. The next was taken from behind a couch in a nice living room. In the center of the picture was the back of a woman's head. The third picture was taken from the front. It was clear from this angle that the woman was dead. Her throat had been cut. In her lap was a small toddler. There was a slash across the toddler's neck as well.

"No. I don't recognize this," Chris said. There was a new, dark seriousness to his demeanor. His voice had lost the playfulness.

"You weren't there, on the night of October 23rd? You didn't jab that knife into that poor, defenseless baby's neck, you brutal, sick, son of a bitch," Detective Benny barked.

"No. I wasn't there," Chris said slowly, meaning every word.

Detective Benny retrieved three more photos from the file. With dramatic care, he laid them next the ones already on the table. The first photo showed two burned bars. The second was of the pummeled body of Anita Dickson. The third and final was of Anita's mangled face and missing eyes. "Do you recognize these?" he asked with grave precision.

"I know the bar."

"Did you set the bar on fire?"

"No."

"But you were there?"

"I heard about the fire and came to watch the firemen put it out."

"Did you know Anita Dickson?"

"Who?"

"Anita Dickson. The woman you beat to death. The woman whose eyes you cut out? Did you know her?"

"I didn't cut anyone's eyes out. And no, I didn't know her."

"Did you know she had a husband?"

"No."

"What about her five year old daughter, Sasha? Did you know she had a five year old daughter? Do you like hurting moms of young kids? You know they had to have a closed casket funeral? Because you destroyed her face so badly. Sasha wept, begging to see her mom again. Is that what gets you off, Mr. Gracanjo? You like hurting moms and watching kids cry?"

Chris' eyes glistened with tears. With soft sorrow he said, "Gracanjo is more of a title."

"I don't give a shit," Detective Benny shot back with fury. "Answer the goddamn question. Did you know Anita Dickson?"

"No, I didn't know her."

"So you didn't drop her body out of a car before you lit the two bars on fire?"

"I didn't light anything on fire."

"You lit a pickup truck on fire today, didn't you?" Benny said. He let the question hang in the air. "So you're saying you didn't light the bars on fire, but you were there?"

"Yes. After the fire started."

"How long after?"

"The buildings were fully engulfed by the time I arrived."

"Was anyone with you?"

"My nephew."

"Your nephew. His name is," Benny checked the notes Rosie had given him. "Jose?"

"Yes."

"Jose what?"

The suspect flashed a small grin. "No. Not what."

"Don't smile at me you dirty, baby-killing, son of a bitch. This isn't a game. What is your nephew's last name?"

"Gracanjo."

"I thought it was more a title."

Chris looked up with a critical glare. "Titles define us. Like Officer-Detective."

"What about the fire a few nights ago? In Fells Point. You and your nephew were there too. Did you light that one?"

"No."

"Was it just the two of you at that one?"

"And another friend, Agnew."

"There wasn't another small man with you?"

"No."

"A man in a fancy suit?"

"No."

"I have witnesses who say they saw you at the fire that night, and that they saw you leave with a short man in a fancy suit."

"I was there. I didn't leave with a small man."

"These same witnesses say they saw you violently kill a group of men and stuff them into the back of your friend Agnew's pickup truck."

"I would never treat a person with violence."

"But you did stuff someone in your truck?"

"Not someone."

"Not someone?"

"Not someone."

"So something? You shoved something in your truck?"

"Yes. We put something in Agnew's truck."

"Do you often refer to people as objects?"

"No, not often."

"So you only refer to people as objects when you beat them, kill them, cut out their eyes, stab their children, or throw them into the back of trucks?"

"I didn't do those things."

"Agnew is telling my partners a different story right now. She's rolling on you."

He smiled. "Good luck with that one."

"When you say you stuffed 'something' in Agnew's truck, those somethings were people."

"No. They were not."

"What were they then?"

After a pause, he replied with a deep sigh, "They were Mardocks."

"What's a Mardock?"

"Nasty strong things with no hair and sharp teeth that get high off human pain. I've got to keep them off the street. They're never here for a good reason."

"Do you see a lot of these creatures roaming the streets?"

"More than two or three at a time are rare. They only come in force when something big is about to go down."

Mencken stared at Chris with confusion. He couldn't tell if the man was playing with Benny or if Chris was genuinely insane.

Benny leaned forward again. "Listen," he said with empathy, "you're in a lot of trouble here. You need to shoot straight with me and maybe I can cut you a deal. If all you're doing is keeping monsters off the street, then maybe we can work something out. I don't like politicians much either. I mean, I don't think anyone is going to disagree with you that the city is a better place with one less of them roaming around. Just shoot straight with me, okay?"

"An interesting metaphor for an officer to use."

"What?"

"Nothing. I am shooting straight with you."

"How many monsters have you 'taken off the street' this week?"

"I don't keep count."

"Estimate it for me."

"It's Thursday? So seven. I'd guess this week there's been seven."

"You've killed seven monsters this week?"

"Um, not really killed. Killing implies an end. I really did something more like pushing their reset button. They don't die. They reincarnate back in their homeland, but for your limited understanding, yeah. I killed seven monsters this week."

Detective Benny continued to pursue her line of questioning, ignoring the random comments. "Did your nephew help you with all of these?"

"Yep. We're a team."

"When you killed the State's Attorney's family, did that count as one take down or three?"

"I didn't do that. And they weren't monsters. They were people. I'm disappointed you don't know the difference. I'm starting to think you lack compassion for humanity, Officer Detective Frank Benny."

"You expect me to believe that," Benny said. "You're trying to tell me that you saw three giant monsters with sharp teeth, sitting in front of a church today, and you decided to do a public service and rid the world of them?"

"No."

Detective Benny brought his emotional levels back under control. "Thank you. I appreciate your honesty. So what really happened at the church today?"

"I told you."

"But then you said 'no'."

""No. I said I don't expect you to believe it."

The Detective raged again. "Goddamn it," he said, smacking the table.

"You need to make up your mind if we are doing this for his sake or if you expect him to damn it. Or are we asking him to damn it for his sake?"

"I've seen enough," Rosie said. She stood and left the observation room. Much to Mencken and Frank's shock, Rosie appeared in the interrogation room a second later.

"Excuse me," she said to Chris. "I'm Detective Jimenez."

"What in the fuck are you doing in here?" Frank barked, but Mencken could tell from the look on his face that he was happy to get some help.

Rosie didn't answer. She stood next to Frank, and looked at Chris. "Listen," she said apologetically. "I'm really sorry. It's just, Frank and I are under a lot of pressure. Our boss is all over us to get these cases wrapped up. But we shouldn't take it out on you. Tell me about State's Attorney Cleveland."

"Okay," Chris said.

"So you know him?"

"No."

"But you said you knew he was a State's Attorney?"

"Yes."

"Did someone order you to kill State's Attorney Cleveland?"

"No."

"Did you know he was holding up a development deal for new condo construction in the inner harbor?"

"No."

"Do you think that's why someone had you kill then?"

"I'm not sure how to answer that."

"Who's paying you to kill people?"

"No one."

"But you admit to killing them?"

"No."

"We have a source that says he saw you attack a different group of men three days ago. How often do you throw groups of men into the back of pickup trucks?"

"Never."

"This is nonsense," Frank mumbled. "I'll have your fucking badge for this."

"We have a source that saw you take three men off the street, beat the hell out of them, and then toss him in your friend Agnew's truck," Rosie said, pressing on.

"You have a lot of sources who speak to my actions," Chris said.

"Our source took a picture of you driving away from the Cleveland's house." Rosie reached in front of Frank, pulled a seventh picture from the file, and placed it next to the others on the table in front of the suspect.

"That Menken Cassie just can't mind his own business," Chris said.

"He is a reporter, it's his job," Rosie said.

"He's not a real reporter," Chris said with a smile.

"He is a real reporter."

"So he's the source?"

"I didn't say that."

"Okay, Officer Detective Frank Benny and Detective Jimenez. You know who you should never trust? A man with a last name for his first name and a woman's name for his last. Talk about not trusting people. And a reporter on top of that. Have you read what he has written about your fellow officers? Officer-Detective Frank Benny, I'm pretty sure you've been featured."

"What are you talking about?" Frank said.

"Have you read what he has written about them? He doesn't think much of your profession. Corruption. Greed. Accepting bribes," Chris said.

"I've read Mr. Cassie's work," Frank said. "But I've got nothing to hide."

"Mr. Cassie does not say nice things about the Baltimore police force," Chris said.

"What Mencken does or does not write about the police force is not the issue here," Rosie said. "You've been arrested for the murder of three people, and are suspected for murdering a council member, his family, and an upstanding member of the community."

"First name basis, huh?"

"What?"

"Speaking of outlandish sources and Mr. Cassie. Mr. Cassie, or Mencken as you call him, wrote a shocking expose a few months ago about corruption in the Eastern District force. He claimed he had an inside source."

"Mr. Gracanjo. You are in serious trouble here," Frank said. "We're going to put you away for life. Do you understand? Do you get what is happening here?"

"Do you?" Chris said.

"Of course I do. I'm the one in charge here. I'm the one that's going to throw you away for the rest of your goddamn life, you baby-killing, son of a bitch." There was less conviction in Frank's voice now.

"Have you found them?" Chris asked Rosie.

"Found what, Chris? What am I supposed to find?" Rosie said, pulling up a chair to the table.

"Bodies. You said I took people. Have you found the bodies?"

"No," Frank said, looking at Rosie.

"Good," Chris said

"Why is that good?" Rosie asked.

"Because if the answer was 'yes', it means we did something wrong," Chris said.

"I guess you did something right, which is why they are called 'disappearances,' rather than murders," Rosie said.

"Do you have names?" Chris asked.

"Names?" Frank asked.

"Names of the people I supposedly took away in Agnew's magic truck."

"We suspect the small man you attacked at the fire is actually this child here," Frank said. The detective removed another photo from the file. This one was a small, rectangular, wallet sized picture of a small brown haired boy. He placed it on the table. "Do you know the Couches? Their son went missing the night of the fire."

"I don't know them," Chris said.

"How long did you stalk him?" Rosie asked.

"Stalk who?" Chris said.

"Jessie. Jessie Couch," Frank said. "The boy you kidnapped. His parents said he was prone to playing dress-up."

"I didn't stalk Jessie Couch," Chris said.

"So you just nabbed him. What? Just grabbed the closest kid to you. Where is he you bastard?" Frank yelled, smacking the table again.

"I've never seen nor had contact with Jessie Couch," Chris said. "I'm sorry he's missing."

"Bullshit," Rosie said.

"I'm sorry?" Chris said.

"Bullshit on all of it," Rosie said. "You know what they do to candy-ass guys like you in the Baltimore prison?

Guys that steal kids? Guys that stab babies? They are going to rape you over and over and over until you don't even remember your name. So for your sake, you need to start talking."

"Ok then," Chris said.

"Ok then, what?" Frank asked, leaning back.

"Ok then, I will explain it all to you."

"Wonderful. Get started," Rosie said.

"Ready?" Chris asked.

"Yeah," Frank said.

"No you're not."

"Yes. Yes we are," Rosie said.

"No. If you were, you would have something to write this down."

"I'm recording it," Frank said.

"You sure about that?" Chris asked.

"Now, please. We're ready now. Let's do this," Rosie said.

"Detective Jimenez, Officer-Detective Frank Benny, there is a place called Midian."

"Where is it?" Frank asked.

"Across the Veil."

"Across the veil, you say? Where is this veil?"

"Here."

"Where? In this interrogation room?"

"Sure. From what I understand, it is pretty much the same as everywhere."

"Ok, then," Rosie said. "So, Midian, tell us about Midian."

"Okay. It's rather boring, which isn't always a bad thing. The weather patterns are really strange. Most people can't get there. It's bigger than Reality, but overlays Reality, so when you're there, the shadow of Reality looks bigger than it actually is. I've heard stories about the Malacandra and Cocytus being at war and Tinker playing a part in it, but I don't really care. You know? As long as they stay out of my city, they can do what they want."

"Who's at war?" Frank asked, leaning back again.

"The monsters. The monsters are at war," Chris said.

"And your city. Where is your city?" Rosie asked.

"Here. Baltimore. I'm charged with Baltimore," Chris said.

"And you see these monsters? You see them in your city?" Rosie said.

"Yep," Chris said.

"What do they look like?" Frank asked.

"Um, well. I've seen five kinds in person. I've heard there are more. The Sinciputs are like freaky, scary little people. They're obsessed with having nice things. They tend to be in charge of strategic planning. The Mardocks are strong and tall, like an NFL linebacker. But they don't have any pigment in their skin. Big, black, swirling eyes. Kind of freaky. The Conculos look the most like us, except they have teeth like a dog and their eyes are like solid crystals. And then there's the Slakes. They're fairly harmless alone. It's when they're in packs that you have to watch out for them. Oh, and the Egrats. They're giant bull like things, but with a face like a pug. I know that sounds nuts. They're usually good-natured, unless someone has stirred them up."

Frank and Rosie exchanged a knowing look.

"And you killed one of these monsters outside the church today?" Frank asked.

"Yeah. Three Mardocks," Chris said.

"And you were hunting one outside State's Attorney Cleveland's house the night he died?" Rosie asked. Her voice was sad.

"A pack actually. Mardocks. At least three," Chris said.

"You sure it wasn't two Mardocks and a small, um, what'd you call it? A small, um, Sinciput?" Rosie asked.

"Yeah. I'm sure," Chris said.

"How are you sure?" Frank asked. He rubbed his eyes in exhaustion.

"I can smell them," Chris said.

"You can smell them," Rosie said.

"Yep. Comes with the job," Chris said.

The look in the Chris' eyes confirmed to Mencken that Chris was being genuine. A deep wave of pity washed over him, threating to release the dam that held his emotions in reserve. He was certain of two things: Chris was insane, and Chris was capable of killing.

Rosie took in a long breath, leaned back in her chair, weaved her fingers together behind her head, closed her eyes, and let her breath go slowly.

"Semper Fi?" the suspect asked.

Rosie jolted forward. "What?"

"Marine?" Chris said, pulling his hand against the cuffs to point at the tattoo on Rosie's forearm.

"What do you know about it?"

"Oh, Gunny. I know all about it."

"Did you serve?"

"I was Recon."

"My little brother is Recon," Rosie said.

"Is he still in?" Chris asked.

"Yeah," Rosie said.

"I was probably about five years before you if I'm guessing your age right. Why'd you get out?"

"Took shrapnel in the leg. Did you see action?"

It occurred to Mencken that PTSD would explain some things about Chris.

The suspect smiled and then said softly, "I'm the Blur."

Rosie sat back in her chair. Her mouth hung open. She looked at Frank. He gave her a confused stare. She stared into the suspect's eyes, watching for tells of a bluff. "You're the Blur," she said, stunned. "The Blur."

The suspect laughed to himself, seemingly embarrassed to be recognized. "Yeah. I'm the Blur."

"Can somebody fill me in here?" Frank said.

But Rosie was in a world of her own thought. "That explains a lot," she said to herself.

"You have no idea," Chris said.

"Explains what? Damn it. Explain what Jimenez," Frank said with frustration.

Rosie stood and walked to the door. "Frank, I'm going to make a call," she explained. "Watch him."

"You can't tell me what to do," Frank said, but he didn't move from his seat.

"Any way you could take these cuffs off, Gunny?' Chris asked.

Rosie turned and said, "Now that I know who you are, not a chance in hell."

For a moment Mencken had been so lost in the conversation, he'd forgotten where he was, but when Rosie pushed open the door, he stood to face her.

"Do you know who the fuck this is?" Rosario demanded pointed at the window. "I mean. This is insane. Do you have any idea what you've fucking got me into?"

"No. I mean. No," Mencken said, taken aback by Rosie's abrasiveness. "I just thought he was a crazy homeless hitman living in the basement of Imani's bar."

"This guy's a fucking legend. He's a fucking Force Recon legend. I want you to picture Rambo. Now imagine someone kicking Rambo's fucking ass. That's who you fucking brought in here. Do you understand? That's who's in cuffs right now."

"So, you think he's the guy? That sounds like the guy," Mencken said with excitement.

Rosie sighed. "I don't know. I mean, this guy, this fucking guy is a killer. He's a black ops myth."

"So you think he's capable."

"Listen, Mencken," Rosie said, pulling herself together. "If he is who he says he is, and I don't know how he couldn't be, because only Recon guys would know the person he just referenced. But if he is the Blur, then fuck yeah he could be our guy." Rosie paused. Mencken could hear her thinking. "And I think he's gone insane," she continued. "I mean, really insane. Which would make sense, because the shit this guy's seen. I don't know how he could be anything but insane."

"Shit."

"Yeah."

"So what now?"

"Well, I'm going to call the VA and see if I can get a shrink down here to make the declaration official and get this guy some help."

"What should I do?"

"I don't know. Go report something. Or go and find his nephew, if that's who that kid really is. If I can get him committed, we'll need social services in on this too. This is a complete shit storm."

CHAPTER TWENTY-ONE

Flinging the two heavy doors open with both hands, Mencken entered Imani's with a renewed swagger. Chris was in custody, they knew who he was, and the case against him was building. Mencken was sure Chris' walls would only hold up so long, then he'd crack and bring the whole Cabal down around him.

Mencken scanned the room. Abby was working the register. Four tables were filled with regulars. Spencer, the local bum, was at his usual spot in the corner, sipping coffee. In the far corner sat Rothman. His giant arms were crossed across his chest and his eyes were closed. He didn't seem to be sleeping though, more like meditating. Imani was behind the griddle, grilling sandwiches. She was humming and dancing to the Bill Withers tune playing softly through the speakers.

Watching Imani made Mencken wonder why he'd come inside. What was he doing here? Did he really want to rub it in Imani's face? Maybe he could find Jose and leave without having to talk to Imani.

Abby waved. He had to go over now. He smiled and walked to the register. "Hey Abby," he said.

"What can I get you?" she asked with a smile.

"Coffee, to go," he said. "And um, have you seen Jose?"

"Nope. He left with his uncle early this morning. They don't really hang around here during the day."

"Oh," Mencken replied. "Alright. Any guess where I might find him?"

"What scoop are you chasing today, Hon?" Imani said with a big smile as she put two plates down on the counter in front of Abby. Both contained beautifully grilled, flatbread sandwiches stuffed with various meats and cheeses.

Mencken winced at the sound of her voice. To his frustration, Abby announced, "He's looking for Jose." She then picked up the plates and left the conversation to deliver them.

"He's out with Chris," Imani said. "They'll probably be back sometime after dinner. What are you having?"

Mencken swallowed and clenched his fists, trying to muster his courage. The last thing he wanted to do was confront Imani about her homicidal family. He hadn't thought about how all of this might impact her. It wouldn't have stopped him from taking Chris down, but he would have stayed away until everything blew over.

"I, um. I need to talk to him about something he and Chris might have seen? I'm chasing a story about a new gang in town."

"What are you having?" she asked again, only half paying attention, reading through the small stack of mail.

"A coffee to go."

She turned, grabbed a cup, and began to fill it. "They're kind of all over the place. We usually meet for lunch, but I don't know where they go before and after." She passed him the cup and a smile. "They'll be back tonight if you want to check back in."

Mencken fished two dollars out of his wallet and passed them over. "I'll try to figure something else out. Thanks anyway," he said.

As Mencken turned to leave a deep base voice filled the room. "You haven't inquired of me." Rothman's voice was so commanding, the whole room turned toward the giant man. His posture hadn't changed. His eyes were still closed. It was as if the voice had come from nowhere.

"You better go over, baby," Imani said. "I haven't heard him speak all day. He's just been sitting there. He must know something."

Mencken watched the huge man, wondering if he knew, wondering if he was upset, wondering if he would kill Mencken right there. Mencken choked down a swallow as he remembered Rothman's powerful hand around his neck. He remembered the helpless sensation of his feet dangling inches above the ground. He remembered panicking for air.

Mencken look around the room again. There were too many witnesses. That wasn't Chris' style, and Rothman was Chris and Jose's guest. Surely Mencken was safe at Imani's. He took the walk across the room, forcing every step to look normal and confident. He pulled out the chair across from the mountain, took a seat, and sipped his coffee.

Rothman didn't move.

"So?" Mencken said.

With his eyes still closed, he replied, "You are the story writer which removed the Lead Gracanjo of Baltimore from his duty?"

"What's that supposed to mean?"

"You squander my time in your verbal jousting. Precious time that I value much too greatly to engage in games of juvenile nonsense."

"Great then. Let's get to it," Mencken said sitting forward. "Why don't you treat me like a man then and look at me when you speak with me."

Rothman smiled. He stretched his neck to the left and right. At the pinnacle of each move, there was a loud pop. He then rolled his shoulders and opened his eyes. The man's deep, dark eyes sent chills down Mencken's spine. The lines in Rothman's forehead were valleys of experience, and the dark worn circles under his eyes looked as though they had been hammered into the man's face by endless scenes of horror.

"I will grant you the modicum of respect, due a man of your questionable profession that has had minor success. Many have tried to remove the Baltimore Gracanjo. Many more powerful than you. And there is something we should discuss." His voice was a low rumble, like a slow train passing through a residential neighborhood in the middle of the night.

"Tell me where I can find Jose?" Mencken demanded.

"This is not what we need to discuss. We need to discuss your behavior in this establishment."

"My behavior?"

"Inquiring after the whereabouts of the young Gracanjo from their benefactor, but not owning your part in the matter, that is a disrespect I could not let pass."

"This is nonsense. You need to tell me where Jose is. It's important that I find him. He's out there all alone. We need to bring him in. Find him a proper home."

"Tell me. Do you understand your part in this? Or are you simply a blind man relieving himself in the road, who accidently pissed on the king?"

Mencken smacked the table in anger and leaned forward. "I know exactly what I'm doing. You and your Cabal, you're going to face justice for what you've done to this city."

Rothman smiled again. "A pissing blind man it is then," he said as he closed his eyes, returning to his previous statuesque state.

Mencken stood. "Are you going to tell me where to find the boy or not?"

"Boy?" Rothman grunted with amusement. "Rest assured in your simple existence, and respect those that carry the heavier burden," Rothman replied. "When there is need of you, you are the one who will be found."

Mencken pointed a threatening finger at the giant. "You're all going down. I'll see you all behind bars." Then he turned and stormed out.

Back on the street, Mencken felt strong again. "That guy deserves to be in jail," he mumbled to himself as he checked his phone. Nothing exciting from Twitter. "Probably sitting in there because he's afraid I was going to catch him too," he grumbled again. Nothing of note in his email either. He thought about texting Rosie but decided against it. She'd seemed scared. No need to add pressure. "She'll call when she's got something," he assured himself. Looking up and down the street, he sucked in the crisp air, letting it fill his cheeks. He pushed it out in a fast rush. Unsure what else to do, he crossed the street to where he'd parked his bike.

"Hey," a high pitched voice called, stopping Mencken before he started the engine. Mencken looked up but saw no one.

"Hey, you. On the wheely thingy," the voice called again.

Mencken found its source this time. Peeking out from an alley between two rowhomes was the small man from the fire. As at the fire, he was dressed to the hilt. He wore shiny, expensive looking black and white leather shoes, a perfectly pressed, pin-striped, three-piece suit, and a small monocle on a gold chain that led to his left breast pocket.

"Come here. Come closer," the tiny man called, waving Mencken forward.

Mencken couldn't pass up a story like this. Who was this tiny man, and what did he want? Mencken dismounted his bike and stepped forward.

The man giggled with excitement. "Yes, yes. It comes. Come here. Come here."

Mencken cocked his head slightly to the side. "What'd you want?" he said.

"I want you to come. I want you to come here," the

man said with irritation. His words shot faster than they should have, firing from his mouth like a machine gun.

Mencken shook his head in disbelief. "Alright," he said, thinking there wasn't anything a man so small could do to him.

Mencken took another two steps forward, when, from the alley to his right, powerful hands grabbed him and lifted him off the ground, yanking him off the street and into the shadows of the alley.

Mencken stared with horror into the face of his captor. The hands held him so tightly, he thought his arms might snap like twigs. The powerful arms belong to a powerful man, unlike any that Mencken had ever seen. The man was hairless. His skin was as white as typing paper. His razor sharp teeth would have been perfectly at home in a shark's mouth, but most terrifying were his eyes. Where the pupil, iris, and sclera should have been, there was a slowly rotating pool of black ooze.

"Don't kill it until I've interrogated it," squeaked the high-pitched voice. It was right behind Mencken.

The monster smiled, its teeth gleaming. It eased Mencken back four inches, and then pulled him forward with incredible force, delivering a powerful head butt. Mencken's world went black.

CHAPTER TWENTY-TWO

Mencken awoke with a gasp of terror. His body ached and his head pounded. He tried to look around, but he was unable to move his head. Everything was blurry, and there was something in his mouth. It was cushiony, absorbing all the moisture like a dry sponge. The return of his consciousness brought with it increasing panic. He tried to move his legs and arms, but they were restrained. He jerked his neck left and right, but his forehead was strapped to something.

Mencken's eyes darted back and forth, searching for an explanation. Slowly, the room came into focus. There were two boarded-up windows across from him. Beams of dust covered light sprang from cracks in the plywood. The air reeked of rot and mold. The walls were bare and dirty. The floor was covered with dirty, yellow carpet. There was no furniture of any kind. He could make out graffiti in his peripheral vision to the right. The tumblers of his mind fell into place. It was an abandoned rowhome. He was on the second or third floor of an abandoned rowhome.

He fought to move his arms and legs again. He could feel the strain of the chair he was in. Forcing his glance as low as his eyes would allow, he could make out the color of duct tape around his wrists. He tried to scream, but whatever was in his mouth stole the sound. Tears formed in his eyes. He was lost. Helpless. Hopeless. He felt the drops slide down his cheeks. He moaned and wept. He knew that no one was coming for him. No one would even begin to look for him for days. He was alone.

There was pounding on the stairs to his right. He strained to look, but whatever was restraining his head refused to give. He tried to scream, but only muffled moans came through.

A door opened. People were coming into the room. He heard deep, low voices muttering to each other. They sounded joyful, entertained. He thrashed against his restraints, trying to scream.

A figure appeared in Mencken's peripheral vision on the left. It was the small man from the fire. Mencken watched in terror as the man removed his coat, folded it gently, and then handed it to someone out of his line of sight.

"Hello," the small man said, stepping in front of Mencken.

Up close, Mencken saw the man for what he was. He wore a large smile, revealing jagged, uneven teeth. His eyes were bigger than they should have been, too large and round for his small head. The monocle looked comically small in comparison. His button down was white. All four buttons of his tightly fitting vest were fastened. His skin was pale and oily. His black, stringy hair was parted down the middle.

Mencken felt a crowd of people behind him. He wasn't sure who or how many, but there was more than one. His instincts told him they were crammed into the back of the room like concert goers in a small space, waiting for a popular band.

"Well, well, well," the small man chimed in a sharp, high pitched voice. His hands were behind his back. He rocked on the heels of his shoes. "You almost had me. I was confused for a moment. Why? Why would you remove the nasty Gracanjo from the field of play? Very trickster of you. Very, wery, nary trickiness, tricksters. You is unknown. Unaccounted for. We haves you now though. Now you will be forthcomings of an account to me, here, on the eve of the moment."

Fresh tears of terror flowed from Mencken's eyes. He thrashed left and right to no avail. He tried to explain, to say he didn't know what the man was talking about, but all that came out was a jumbled, mumble of mushed sound.

"You's turn to speak has not come. You will be asked to speak in a moment. Right now you is to remain still. You should be perfectly-werfectly stilly for Gilly. Still and silent for Gilly the Glorious. This is me," the small man said bowing. "Gilly Gilifix the Glorious, sent by Azo the Coming Conquer to prepare the larger than normal portal. Sent and will succeed. Regardless of you's tricks," he said, jamming a finger in Mencken's face. Mencken tried to pull away, but again found himself unable to move more than a few centimeters.

"Now," the small man-thing continued, stepping back again. "Nows yous will tell us why. Why is it that tricky-tricksters has removed the Gracanjo from the field of battle? Why is the bishop out of play? One does not gain the checks and the mates without the use of the bishops. Why then, would the silliest trickster pawn, an unknown pawn, unseen because of you's insignificance to the game – why would such a trickier trickiest remove the bishop?"

The man stood, waiting for Mencken to answer.

Another tear ran down Mencken's cheek.

In a whirlwind of rage, the small man raced toward Mencken. Pointing his finger in Mencken's face, he screamed, "You will answer when Gilly speaks. You will answer me!"

The small man-thing's breath stunk of death and sorrow. Mencken wept and tried to speak, to explain that he didn't understand, but again the sound was lost.

The blow to Mencken's midsection was quick and painful. The sharp, but powerful jab from the tiny man made Mencken's breath flee his lungs. Vomit rose in his throat. He choked on the stomach acid. "The trickster will answer!" the man-thing screamed again with its high, shrill voice.

Mencken closed his eyes and wept. Moaning for this nightmare to end.

There was a deep rumble of a voice from behind Mencken. The small man looked past Mencken, nodding his head in agreement. Then he looked back at Mencken with an apologetic smile. "Gilly apologizes," he said. "I did not realize the trickster could not speak with the gag still in its mouth."

The small man reached behind Mencken's head. Mencken felt a tugging and then a release. A heavy cloth ball fell from his mouth. It dangled at the end of a string Gilly held up for Mencken to see. Mencken drew air through his mouth. His tongue and soft palate were on fire. He could still taste the cloth in his mouth. Remnants of fuzz covered his tongue and the insides of his cheeks.

"It should speak now," Gilly said.

"I. I um." Mencken didn't recognize his own voice. It was dry and hoarse.

"I um. I um. I um. I um," Gilly raged in rapid fire. "No. No. No. You speaks wordy words now. You explains you's trickster ways."

"I um," Mencken said before the sharp blow to his chest cleared the air from his lungs, leaving behind nothing but pain.

"Say 'I um' again and Gilly will cut you's heart out," Gilly said.

"I don't. I don't know anything," Mencken cried.

"Lies," Gilly declared calmly. "Lying lies from a lying mouth of lyingness. You will tell Gilly the Glorious why you had the Gracanjo taken off the field."

"You mean Chris?" Mencken cough. "Chris?"

"I care not of the Gracanjos names."

"I thought. I thought Chris was. I thought."

"I thought. I thought. I thought," Gilly chanted in anger. "You does not think. You explains. You tells. You speaks truth. No more 'I thoughts'."

"I had him arrested. For. For killing those men."

A roar of deep and low laughter tore through the crowd behind Mencken.

Gilly smiled. "So you is an accidental surprise for Gilly – how do you say – coincidence?"

"I. I guess so."

The blow to Mencken's jaw was powerful. It forced his already pounding head to pull against his restraints. He felt his jaw muscles fight to stay in socket. His teeth rattled. Blood flowed freely from his nose and lip, clogging his breath.

"You does not guess," Gilly said. "You knows. You must knows. You must not guess. Now, will the Gracanjo return for the fight? Gilly the Gracious gives you a hint. You should prepare you's answer before yous speaks. Gilly does not want to break you's jaw yet. We have more to discuss."

"He's locked up," Mencken said. "He's not getting out any time soon. Agnew too. The, um, the girl? She's locked up too."

Gilly did a victory dance, pumping his legs up and down while thrusting his fists into the air. Then turning back to Mencken he explained, "The wounded Gracanjo from the north is of no concern. We've already taken the life of its partner. And Canthos has disabled her leg."

There was a pride filled grunt behind Mencken.

"The Rothman is still a concern. But even he and the small one cannot take our force as it stands now," Gilly continued, now looking at the ceiling as if he were thinking out loud. Then, turning back to Mencken, Gilly said, "Thank you. Thank thanks for removing the two from the field. Gilly the Glorious will remember you's helpfulness."

"Can I. Can I go?" Mencken said, feeling a shard hope for the first time.

Gilly laughed. "No Nos. We must bring you more pain so my force can feed. They will eat the essence of you's suffering and prepare for the final battle. But, you has my word that no unnecessary suffering will occur. We will only extract what we need, then we will end you's life. This is fair. Fair for all you's have done for the army of Azo the Coming Conqueror."

Mencken felt tears in his eyes again.

Gilly looked past him and commanded, "Open its head."

Mencken felt the restraints around his forehead fall loose. Frantically, he looked left and right, desperate to see more of where he was and what was behind him. In his peripheral vision, he caught glimpses of pale, tall, muscular things wearing loose-fitting shirts and sweat pants. Mencken could count three, maybe four. They were difficult to distinguish from one another without turning around completely.

Strong, cold hands gripped his head, forcing his eyes forward. The fingernails felt like steel daggers against his skin. The small man was in front of him again, smiling. The hands on his temples forced Mencken's head back. Standing above him, smiling down at him, was one of the musclebound, monsters. Mencken had forgotten the eyes – the swirling, black pools of terror. Fear raced through Mencken's blood. He fought to get away, thrashing with all his might. The monster above him laughed in reply.

"Hurry, hurry," Gilly said. "We must go. If you want to feed, you need to do it quickly."

The beast shifted its grip on Mencken's head, forcing two fingers into the top of Menken's mouth and two into the bottom. Then, with gentle force, the pale creature pried Mencken's mouth open.

Mencken tried to scream, but what came out was more of a moan. He clinched his eyes shut, hoping the entire experience would vanish, hoping he would pass out or fall asleep, hoping something would allow him to escape whatever was about to come.

He felt pressure on his knees. Something, someone was standing on him. Shadows shifted. There were two small fingers in his mouth, feeling each one of his teeth. They were dirty and dry. The fingers stopped on a lower left molar.

Mencken moaned, pleading, begging, wanting it to stop. Droll slipped from both sides of his mouth.

"Everyone gather round," Gilly said. "Its pain will be sharp, but quick."

More shadows arrived. Mencken sensed the crowd gather around him. He moaned again, trying to verbalize a "No! Please!" without the use of his mouth or tongue. Tears poured freely from his eyes.

The small fingers found a molar. Sharp nails pierced his gum. Mencken screamed. The fingers yanked up. Blood filled Mencken's mouth. The warm, thick liquid pooled in his throat. He began to choke on it. He hoped it would drown him.

The hands holding his mouth open forced his head to the left. Blood drained from his throat, down the inside of his cheek, and escaped the corner of his lip, dripping to floor.

"One more before we kills it?" Gilly asked with enthusiasm.

There was a deep, satisfied mummer from the crowd.

Mencken's head was forced back into position. His muscles were numb and powerless. He responded like a stuff animal being tossed around by a child. Everything was blurry. Blood began to fill his throat again. The room spun. He prayed for death.

The fingers returned, but this time to the other side. Again, the small, sharp nails pierced his gums. Again a tooth was yanked from his head. Again, blood flowed. And again, his head was forced to the side, so the blood could drain.

The hands released his head. There was talking, but Mencken could no longer decipher what was being said. He knew the words, but his mind was too fuzzy to comprehending what they meant. His heart pounded in his head. Blood continued to run from his mouth. He sat, limp, his head hanging where the hands had left it. He closed his eyes, and passed out.

He was awoken to small hands at his feet. "No more," he moaned. "Please. Please, no more." His eyes struggled to gain focus again. He could make out a single shape in front of him. His mouth was caked full of dried blood. His neck was sore, and his head still pounded with the beat of his heart.

"It's alright," a kind, young voice said Mencken recognized it, but couldn't yet place it. "It's over. They're gone. We drew them away."

Mencken felt his feet freed from their restraints. Then his wrists. He lay limp, still unable to gather the energy to move. He closed his eyes, incapable of caring who was in front of him.

There was a warm hand on his forehead. Then two hands gently lifted his chin. Mencken opened his eyes again. A face. A kind face. A young face. Jose. It was Jose. A new river of tears filled Mencken's eyes.

"Rothman," Jose called to the stairs. "He's up here. I need you. He's too big for me to carry."

"Jose," Mencken said through tears of relief. The words were like daggers in his mouth.

The boy's voice was filled with sorrow. He stroked Mencken's cheek. "We're going to get you out of here. Go back to sleep. You're safe. You're safe now."

Mencken sighed, and the world went dark again.

CHAPTER TWENTY-THREE

Mencken was aware of his breathing. The air was tart and cold. He shivered. His mouth felt like it was stuffed with bitter, dry cake. The sun was bright, he could feel its warmth on his eyelids. The metal beneath his head was cold. He took a deep breath, holding the cold air in his lungs, then exhaling slowly. With his senses coming back to him, he opened his eyes. Above him was a blue sky with tuffs of white clouds.

"How are you feeling?" a voice in front of him asked.

Mencken struggled to sit up. His limbs and ribs hurt. Blood rushed into his head as he rose, harkening the return of his headache. Mencken looked around. He was sitting on the hood of an old beige car. He was on the top floor of a parking garage. The car he sat on was pulled up to the four-foot tall, concrete wall that went around the top floor. Sitting on the wall in front of him, with his back to Mencken and his legs hanging over the edge of the wall, was Chris.

"How's your head?" Chris asked.

Mencken wasn't sure how to answer. He wondered what was going to happen next. Was this man going to throw him off the ledge? Did he carry a grudge? Was he a man at all, or one of those things, one of those horrible monsters? Was this even real? Mencken wasn't sure of anything. He laid back down on the hood of the car, in surrender.

Chris laughed. "I bet you have a lot of questions. We've got a few minutes before the others show. I'll tell you what I can, but I can't promise it will make a whole lot of sense." He swung his feet back over the wall to face Mencken. "Seriously. You've got about ten minutes. Ask away."

"How'd you escape?"

"I didn't. I've got some high-up friends who understand my life. They came and let me out shortly after you left."

"Are you going to kill me?"

Chris laughed. "No. We don't hurt people. It's one of our rules."

"Where's Jose?"

"He and Agnew went to pick up Rothman's weapons. Rothman's particular about his weapons."

"Who do you work for?"

"It's complicated. To be honest, I'm not sure. Whoever it is, I don't think it's human."

Mencken sat in silence for a minute. "You promise to be honest?"

"I said I would."

"Did you kill Anita Dickson?"

"No."

"Did you kill the Clevelands?"

"No. But I was there."

"Why?"

"On this side of the Veil, the um – we'll just call them monsters for now to keep it simple. The monsters are like drug addicts. They have to get a fix at least once a day or they start going through withdrawal. The Mardocks get those especially bad. We'd been tracking a trio of them all day. They kept giving us the slip. We caught up with them outside the Clevelands' house."

"Get a fix?"

"Mardocks, the strong, pale ones, get high on human pain and suffering. It's an upper for them."

"Is that why the small dude pulled my teeth out?"

"Yep. They're getting pumped up for battle."

"Was that little one a Mardock?"

"No. That's a Sinciput. It can be confusing at first, but you'll get it."

"Did he get high off my pain too?"

"No. Those little bastards get off on seeing plans succeed. And it's hard to tell if it's a high like the Mardocks, or if they're just fucking nuts."

Mencken sighed. He watched a cloud in the sky. It was thin and moving slowly. He felt like it might disappear in a strong wind. Would the world notice? He reached into his mouth and pulled out two blood-soaked cotton swabs. A fresh trickle of blood began to pool in his mouth. He spit it out toward the side of the car.

"So you're not a hitman for the Cabal?" Mencken said.

Chris turned back, his legs hanging over the side of the wall. "Not sure what the Cabal is, but I'm not a hitman," he said.

"You're some kind of superhero."

"No."

Mencken sat up and spat blood again. It was warm in his mouth. He liked it. It reminded him he was alive. "What do you mean 'no'? You walk around fighting monsters every day."

"Superheroes are in comic books. I'm part of something ancient. An order if you will."

"The Grand-cano."

Chris laughed softly to himself. "It's pronounced Gra-con-joe."

"What's your real last name?"

"It used to be Parker. When you accept the job, the old life goes away. Your name goes with it."

"Why?"

Chris smiled. "Gracanjo don't live long. We usually get the call in our twenties. Few of us see our thirties. I'm considered an old man."

"If you're not fighting crime and protecting people, what's the job, exactly?" Mencken said, leaning back on his elbows. He spat more blood to the right. The trickle was slowing. He didn't know whether to believe the man or not. All he was sure of was that a maniacal elf with a bunch of pale, muscle-bound, freaky-eyed monsters had just torn two teeth out of his head.

"We're like guard dogs. There are two of us in every major city. The monsters cross the Veil, and we make them regret it."

"The Veil?"

"They're from another place. Another world, I guess. It lies on top of ours. The thing that separates us from them is called 'the Veil.' They cross it. We make them pay for it. That's the job. When you're in their world, you can see ours. It's like." Chris paused to think. "On their side we look like ghosts. But not just the people. Everything. They can see everything. But we look like a mist."

Mencken snorted a small laugh.

"I know. It's a lot. But you're smart. You can handle it."

"So if they can see us there, why can't we see them here?"

"I don't know." Chris let his head fall and he sighed. "Some can. I can," he said softly.

"You can what?"

Chris' voice was hollow and lost. "I can see them. They're smaller than in person. I think it is because their world is bigger than ours, so when you lay them on top of each other their world has to shrink to match. But I see them. I see them everywhere I go."

Mencken felt tinge of sorrow for the strange man on the ledge. He wondered how long Chris had been living in this surreal hell of monsters and other worlds. "Does Jose see them too?"

"Not until they cross the Veil," Chris said. "I'm the only one who sees both sides. Sometimes we get special gifts. If we take on the job during moments of extreme violence."

Mencken sat forward and stared down at his feet. The shroud of sorrow around Chris was making the man increasingly difficult to watch. "You said twenties. Jose is young then."

"He was called early," Chris sighed. "Too early. My first partner was the guy that trained me – Carl. Such an asshole. Then I went through a string of partners. None of them lasted long. Then came Jose. He was called up younger than usual."

"Does he have a super power?"

"They're more like curses."

"Does he have curse then?"

"Yeah. He accepted the call in the middle of violence too, so he sees people for who they really are."

"Undecided."

"What?"

"That's what he called me the first time he met me. Undecided. What does that mean?"

"You'd have to ask him."

"Is he really your nephew?"

"Sort of. I knew his dad. We served together."

"As Gray-banjos?"

"Gra-con-joe. Gracanjo. Get it right. And no. As Marines."

Mencken stood. His legs were shaky. They felt like they might buckle beneath him. Resting his forearms on the wall, he leaned on the wall next to Chris. Looking out, he knew exactly where they were. This was the Johns Hopkins' parking garage off Broadway. They were facing west, toward Interstate 83 and its path through the middle of the city. "You've got a thing for parking garages,"

Mencken said.

"They make good lookout towers."

"What do you see now?"

Chris took a deep breath. "Azo's army is camped there." He pointed in the direction of City Hall. "They've been there for over a week. A couple thousand of them from what I can tell."

"Azo?"

"He's kind of a rogue general. It was his strike team you met earlier today."

"What does he want?"

"Rothman says he's looking for some kind of magic box. I don't know, and I don't care."

"If he has an army, why doesn't he just cross the, um, the Veil thingy and take what he wants? I mean there is only four of you Grand-Canyons."

"Gracanjos. Gra-con-joes. And the portals across the Veil are small. They only fit one or two at a time. He's been trying to sneak his army through slowly, but we've held them back so far. And don't call Rothman a Gracanjo. He might hurt you."

"What about Agnew? Is she one of you?"

"Yeah. She and Melody came down from Philly to help out."

Mencken stared to the west. He tried focusing and unfocusing his eyes, like a kid in a mall trying to decipher a Magic Eye puzzle. All he saw was the city at the end of the day. Cars passing one another. People walking about. Nothing out of the ordinary.

Mencken felt a pit in his stomach. Time to address the big issue. "Sorry I had you arrested," he said, sheepishly.

"It's fine. You didn't know. And you paid for it."

"Thanks for being understanding."

"I'm good. But Agnew. She's kind of pissed at you. You know, since your little stunt got her truck torched and all."

Mencken grunted. "It was a piece of shit anyway. Does

Imani believe all of this?"

"Her uncle was one of ours. He was stationed in Boston."

"So what now?" he said. Before the words finished sliding from his mouth, there was noise on the ramp behind them. Mencken turned to look. Jose, Rothman, and Agnew were coming toward them. They weren't dressed like they were going to battle. No armor. No shields. No visible weapons. Jose and Agnew were both in gray sweat pants and t-shirts. Rothman wore flowing black pants and a skin tight black top. He carried a pair of black, forearm length sticks in his right hand.

"Any movement?" Rothman called.

"They're lining up," Chris replied, hopping down from the wall.

The trio arrived at the car. "We should take up offensive positions," Rothman said. "Can you tell from what direction they will enter?"

"Hey Mencken," Jose said, waving.

"Hey, kid," Mencken replied. "Thanks for pulling me out of there."

"Sorry we didn't get there sooner," Jose said with an apologetic shrug.

"I'll know when we get closer," Chris said to Rothman. "I can't tell from this distance."

"How many?" Agnew asked.

"A couple thousand," Chris replied. "And they have Egrats. At least fifty."

"Good," Rothman said. "They'll clog the hole. Only one will fit at a time. It'll create a bottleneck. If Azo deploys his standard tactics, well face Mardocks and Slakes first. The Egrats will come last. He'll try to push us back to create time for them to join the battle. He deployed the same strategy in the third battle for Constantinople."

"How that turn out?" Agnew asked.

"All were lost save me, the city fell, and I was forced to flee across the Bosporus. We reengaged in the field of

Elaia. There we were victorious. Azo had achieved his objective, though, and had already fled the field of battle. As he knows I am present, he will most likely attempt to use my memory of the defeat to demoralize us."

As Rothman was talking, Jose whispered to Mencken, "An Egrat's a huge, eight-foot-tall beast with horns like a bull."

"Thanks," Mencken whispered back.

"Just don't want you to get lost," Jose said with a smile.

"Oh," Mencken said looking down at the teen, "I'm way past lost."

"Anything else about that battle we need to know then?" Agnew asked.

Rothman looked into the air, trying to recall. "There was a preemptive strike force then, as this time. They took positions in front of the portal, creating a fifteen-yard perimeter. A steady stream of fresh troops poured from the opening. Two at a time."

"Sorry about having you arrested," Mencken whispered to Agnew.

"You owe me a new fucking truck, asshole," Agnew whispered back, her eyes filled with rage.

"What turned the tide in his favor?" Chris asked.

"Geography. Constantinople was built on seven hills. Azo made his entrance at the top of the third hill, giving them the advantage of higher ground. We were overcome from the sheer exhaustion of battling uphill."

"City Hall isn't on a hill," Mencken said.

The group pondered this for a moment together.

"Azo knows I can see him," Chris said.

"You think he means to change the field of battle at the final moment." Rothman replied.

"With no buildings or traffic in the way, a jog from City Hall to the top of Federal Hill would be easy," Jose remarked.

"Does he have spies on us?" Rothman asked.

"Yeah," Chris said, peering over the wall. "There's two

Slakes at the entrance of the garage. They've been following my car all day."

"A Slake looks kind of like a cross between a rat and a man," Jose whispered.

"Thanks," Mencken said.

"Long noses. Long tails. No hair or fur though. Just skin, like a man," Jose said.

"Weird," Mencken replied.

"Yep," Jose said. "They're creepy. They slide on their bellies. Jump around a lot. I hate them."

"Focus, young one," Rothman said without looking at Jose.

"If it were me," Agnew said. "I'd open the portal at the crest of the hill, give my troops a running start through the park, and then have them pour down the hill toward the harbor. I could assemble my army at the bottom of the hill. Pressing down on you wouldn't be a problem. The hill is so steep, I could almost jump over you."

They all sat in silence, pondering the problem.

"Okay," Chris said, finally breaking the silence. "I have a plan. But first we need to lose our tails."

CHAPTER TWENTY-FOUR

"This is stupid," Mencken said as he pulled the car down the garage ramp.

"Why?" Jose said with a smile. He sat in the front passenger seat.

"Because it is not going to work," Mencken said.

"Why'd you say that?"

Mencken took another turn. "Because Chris and I look nothing alike."

"Doesn't matter," Jose said, waving Mencken off.

"He's what? Five-six? Five-seven? I'm six-foot-one."

"They won't notice."

"He's got a full head of hair. I'm bald."

"Doesn't matter."

"I've got a beard. He's clean-shaven."

"So."

"I'm black. He's white."

"Okay," Jose said, shifting in his seat to face Mencken. "Here's the deal. These things, they don't die. They just reincarnate back in their home realm. And that doesn't happen often, so most of them are really old. And I mean like, really old. Thousands of years old."

"So?"

"So they don't see us as individuals. We don't live long enough for them to care about our differences. We're like blades of grass to them. Do you know the difference between each blade of grass?"

"No," Mencken said, pulling up to the exit.

Jose looked forward. "Exactly. Besides, these two idiots are just following the car anyway. Make sure you wave," he said. "They'll notice that."

"They're on your left," Chris' voice said through the cell-phone speaker. "Driver's side." The phone rested in the space under the parking brake between Jose and Mencken.

Mencken pulled to the exit and stopped. "This is stupid," Mencken said through a forced smile. He waved to the invisible monsters outside his window. Then he pulled the car forward and into the street.

"It worked," Chris said. "They're following you. Take your time. We'll see you at the Hill." Then the phone went dead.

They drove in silence for a moment. Then Mencken turned onto Caroline Street. "I need you to explain something to me," he said.

"Just one thing?"

"Undecided," Mencken said, his eyes on the road. "What'd you mean, undecided?"

"I meant, you don't know who you are yet," Jose replied. There was a simplicity to his voice, as if Mencken's question was the easiest thing in the world to answer.

"I know who I am."

"You're at a crossroad," the teen replied.

"This is stupid. I don't know why I even brought this up."

Jose shifted in his seat pulling his feet up to sit cross-legged. "You're trying to decide where you are going to find fulfillment: by pursuing your own glory or as a member of a family. Right now, you're undecided."

"You don't know anything about me."

"The touch doesn't lie," Jose said, facing forward again.

They drove in silence for another minute. Mencken turned right onto Fayette. Mencken broke the silence, "Do you think they're still following us."

"Yep," Jose said. "Slakes aren't so smart. Azo likes them because they follow orders."

"Huh," Mencken replied. Changing the subject he asked, "That night at Imani's, when Chris lost it?"

"Rough fight. We lost Melody," Jose seemed suddenly distant at the girl's name. "Azo lost more though. He was pissed, so he followed us home."

They took another block in silence. Again, Mencken broke it. "You don't know what you are talking about, by the way," he said. "I'm not all about my own glory, and I can be about me and be part of a family. They aren't mutually exclusive."

"Okay."

Mencken slowed so they would get the red light at Central Street. "You're just a damn kid. What do you know?"

"I know stuff," Jose said.

"I can have both," Mencken said, pulling the car forward.

"Okay," Jose said.

"This is some life you've got, kid."

"It's really more of calling."

"It's nonsense," Mencken said. "Make-believe insanity."

"Was that make-believe that pulled your teeth out?"

They crossed President Street. "It's only a few more blocks now," Mencken said.

"I know," Jose said. "This is my city."

"Right," Mencken said. "I forgot you walk an ultra-marathon every day." He turned the car on Gay Street. City Hall appeared on the right. The white dome and marble steps looked stately and powerful, like something from a different time, when politicians were philosophers.

On the large green mall in front of the marble steps, stood three pale, weight-lifter looking monsters. They were incredibly out of place among the passing suits on cell phones. Mencken thought back to the black, swirling eyes staring down at him and shivered.

"Pull the car up there," Jose said, pointing to an empty parallel parking spot.

Mencken followed instructions. "Now what," he said as Jose opened the passenger door.

"Now you wait in the car," Jose said loudly as he walked around the car. From his back pocket he pulled a pair of black, fingerless gloves. Mencken watched in awe as the teen put the gloves on and then closed his fists. Two translucent, blue, circular blades materialized from the gloves covering the back of the teen's hands, extending a half-inch past his knuckles.

The monsters saw Jose coming from across the mall. One of them pointed its sharp finger at the boy and gave orders to the other two. They turned and walked to meet the teen. The horrible smiles they wore told the story of the violence they intended to commit on the teenager.

Mencken pushed his car door open and stepped into the street. He didn't have a plan. He just knew he couldn't let the young boy face these beasts alone. They would tear the small teen apart in seconds. Mencken jogged a little, trying to catch up to Jose.

Passersby stopped to watch the confrontation, aware that something was about to happen but confused as to what they were preparing to witness.

"Wait," Mencken called to Jose. "Wait for me," he said. Jose was only fifteen yards from the beasts now. Mencken could see the smiles on the monsters' lips. Their sharp teeth gleamed with delight as their intended prey walked confidently toward them.

Jose did not turn around. Rather, at ten yards out, he broke into a sudden run. It surprised the towering beasts, causing them all three to come to a stop.

Jose closed the gap quickly. The one in the middle sprang forward with both arms, hoping to grab hold of the teen. Jose ducked under its arms. Planting his left foot, Jose delivered an uppercut with this right fist. The blow contained shocking power. Jose connected with the monster's jaw, knocking the massive beast backward. The blue circle on Jose's fist split the beast's chin like an axe splits firewood. Black ooze splattered in all directions. The monster fell backward with a scream.

Pivoting on his right foot, Jose swung hard with his left, hitting the second monster in the back of the knee. The beast fell with a scream.

Jose completed his three-hundred-and-sixty degree spin with a sharp left jab to the third monster's face. The beast's mangled face sprayed a shower of black ooze over Jose.

With all three monsters down, Jose went to work. Standing over the first, which was writhing on its back, Jose separated the beast's head from its body with a crushing, downward right punch. Moving to the second, which was holding its severed knee and shouting in pain, Jose delivered a left jab to the face. Again, the blue blades on his hands cut through the monster's flesh and bone.

Jose turned to finish off the third, but it lay motionless, face down on the ground. He kicked it with his right foot. It didn't respond. Satisfied, Jose turned a walked back toward Mencken. The teen was covered in the black gunk. It was splattered across his face and clothes.

Mencken, like nine other passersby, was frozen with horror. He'd never witnessed such efficient and effective violence before. He no longer perceived the thing walking toward him as a short, Hispanic teen. This thing, this Gracanjo, was a monster of a different breed.

"Let's go," Jose said, walking past Mencken. "We've got to get to the hill to help the others."

Aware he was standing with his mouth hanging open, Mencken said, "Oh. Yeah. The hill. We need to get you and those blue things to the hill." He then ran after Jose.

Back in the car, Jose picked up the cell phone and quickly dialed a number. "Yeah, Ernie. I need a cleanup on the lawn of City Hall. I know. I know Ernie, but I'm too covered in it. I couldn't burn it myself. Yes, there were bystanders. Can you just take care of it? Thanks." He hung up the phone and smiled at Mencken. "Can't believe they only left three," he said. "They must be saving everyone else for the assault."

Mencken pulled the car onto the street. "Who's Ernie?" he asked.

"Ernie's our Relay. Now hurry," Jose said, wiping the black sludge from his eyes. "It's probably already started."

CHAPTER TWENTY-FIVE

Mencken caught his first glimpse of the battle from the corner of Key Highway and Battery Avenue. Three small figures stood on Federal Hill facing a glowing pink circle at the crest of the hill. Pale, strapping warriors poured from the hole, two-by-two.

Jose pounded the dashboard anxiously, yelling, "Get there. Come on. Get there."

The fight was happening on the north side of the hill. The grassy, three story slope was as steep as the nosebleed section of a professional football stadium. The hill was broken in the middle by a sidewalk. The bottom of the hill emptied onto Key Highway. The top of the hill was flat. Along the top, following the hill's crest, was a circular, brick walking path with green, wooden benches every ten feet. Inside the brick walkway was a large grassy space and a playground with climbing equipment shaped like a pirate ship. The north-facing rim was decorated with a Civil War era cannon, a giant American flag, and two small memorials to Baltimore's war heroes.

At the top of the hill, Mencken slowed to take a better look at the fight. The pink circle he had seen from the road was swirling next to the cannon. It was six feet in diameter, just big enough for two of the massive monsters to step through. A steady stream of Mardocks marched through the portal. Agnew, Rothman, and Chris had taken their stand five feet downhill from the swirling circle. They fought on an incline, using their funnel formation to meet and contain the monsters the moment they stepped through the portal. Rothman imposing physique framed the bottom of the V, taking the brunt of the assault and receiving anything the other two deflected toward him. Agnew and Chris worked the left and right edge of the portal. Within seconds of stepping onto the grassy slope, the monsters met their end at the hands of the three heroes. Their broken and lifeless bodies were discarded down the hill. A trail of fifty black-blood stained corpses already littered the bottom half of the slope and were beginning to pile up at the mid-point sidewalk.

Mencken was so entranced by the scene on the hill, he almost didn't notice when Jose threw open the door and jumped from the passenger seat into the street. The small teen ran up the hill toward the action. Fifteen yards from the car, Jose turned back to yelled to Mencken, "Get out of here. Find somewhere safe." His torso and face were illuminated in a faint blue from the glowing, laser like blades on his gloves. After delivering his message, Jose turned and sprinted to join his cohort.

Mencken was in a daze. The scene before him was too much to walk away from. It was like nothing he'd ever seen, like nothing he'd ever imagined. He threw the car into park and stepped into the street. Vehicles streamed by him on the left, honking their horns, too busy with their own lives to stop and notice the scene in front of them, but Mencken couldn't turn his eyes away.

Chris was on Rothman's right. He fought with his bare hands, throwing and breaking combatants much like Jose had done on the lawn of City Hall. He ducked punches and lunges, striking back with fierce, deadly blows before his opponents could respond. His reflexes seemed inhuman. He sidestepped a swipe from on oncoming beast, leveraged the momentum and broke its arm. As the beast screamed in pain, Chris extended both hands in a smooth motion and halted the agonizing moan by snapping the monster's thick neck and simultaneously discarding its body behind him while ducking the attempted strike of the next Mardock running through the portal.

Agnew, on Rothman's left, fought more like a boxer. Left foot forward, right foot back, fists curled up to both protect and attack. She threw power filled jabs, crosses, and upper cuts to anything that came near. She lacked the grace of motion that Chris and Jose displayed, but she was filled a furry and fire unequaled by the other two. Every punch connected with crippling power, demolishing assailants with a single blow. On contact there were explosion of black ooze. Only a few beasts needed a second strike. The rare pause she took from her cadence of hammering was an occasional sideways sweep of a foot to clear the area beneath her of fallen victims.

Rothman was the most terrifying being on the hill that day. He held the center of the siphon, catching any beast that made it past the others and receiving all the monsters they deflected toward him. Each hand wielded a black polished rod the length of his forearm. The ends of the posts were capped with a pointed metallic tip. Dead bodies of monsters flowed from him like water around a rock. With his right, he plunged his stick through the eye of one attacker. As he discarded the enemy with the flick of his wrist, he jammed the left stick into the chin of a second assailant. The force of the blow sending the beast rolling to the right, and tumbling down the hill.

Jose arrived at the battle line, taking up a position between Rothman and Agnew. Like Chris, he dodged and replied to the attacks with deadly efficiency. Unfortunately, his small stature was a disadvantage on the slope. Mencken noticed that often Jose was forced to first take out the beasts at the legs, and then strike their throats or faces as they fell.

A horn blared as a passing truck almost took off Mencken's car door. The noise and rush of wind woke Mencken from the scene. As he turned to yell at the truck, something caught his eye. It was Gilly. The tiny man-thing in the suit was on the left corner of the hill, playing with shiny metal rods. Mencken squinted. The little beast seemed to be assembling something.

Mencken yelled to Jose, "Hey! Jose! Look!" But the boy was too far away and too engrossed in combat to hear. Mencken screamed again, but the foursome did not break their focus.

Mencken looked again to the well-dressed monster. Gilly was gleeful, smiling and laughing to himself. A rock formed in Mencken's gut. He knew anything that would make Gilly happy was bad news for the heroes on the hill. Swallowing his fear, he jumped back in his car. Adrenaline surged through his veins. The pedal was mashed down and tires squealed as Mencken raced to the far corner of the hill and turned right on Covington Street. He whipped it into an empty parking spot in front of the Visionary Art Museum.

Jumping from his vehicle, he looked up the steep east side of the hill. It was peaceful. From this side, you'd never know a battle was being waged beyond the crest. He slammed his car door and ran. It was slow going. His legs ached after a few strides, but he forced himself upward, knowing that he had to stop Gilly. He couldn't let that little teeth-stealing asshole turn the tide.

At the top of the hill, Mencken leaned on his knees and sucked air. His lungs hurt. His mouth ached. His neck throbbed. He scanned the park. It was quiet and empty. Chris had said they would get there early and clear it. Mencken wondered what they had done to chase off all the pedestrians. He could see the back of the pink circle. Nothing came from it. It sat, like a big pink wall, blocking any view of the carnage on the other side.

There was a cackle to Mencken's right. It brought him back to his senses. He remember why he'd run up the hill in the first place. Looking over, he saw Gilly. The small man was still dancing about, fiddling with the shiny pieces of metal. Mencken could tell that Gilly was assembling something, but he had no idea what. Courage filled Mencken's heart. "Hey!" he screamed, walking with authority toward the Sinciput. "You! You took my teeth, you little bastard!"

Gilly looked up, smiled, and clapped rapidly. "You comes to play. You comes to play!" the monster sang.

Mencken lunged, reaching for the little beast with both hands, intending to choke the life from it, but Gilly was faster than Mencken anticipated. Without dropping the two shiny rods, the little monster stepped toward Mencken, grabbed his arm, and bit down on Mencken's wrist. Pain surged through Mencken's body. Gilly's teeth were like knives. Mencken's blood filled Gilly's face. In the split second it occurred to Mencken that Gilly was intending to bite straight through, to take a chunk out of Mencken's left arm. Reflexively, Mencken pounded Gilly's face with his right fist. Once. Twice. Three times before Gilly let go.

Mencken feel to his knees, holding his gushing forearm and applying pressure to stop the bleeding. Tears filled his eyes. His heart pounded with pain. He sobbed uncontrollably, realizing that in seconds, he'd lost. He didn't want to be like Melody. He didn't want to be the one the foursome mourned after the battle.

Gilly leaned in close, coming almost nose to nose with the weeping Mencken. Gilly's mouth, cheeks, and white shirt were coated in red. The beast smiled at Mencken, showing its blood-stained teeth. "You should stay here," Gilly said with glee. "Gilly the Glorious will put these downs and thens comes back for yous with empty hands. Okay?"

With all his might, Mencken pulled back and thrust his forehead forward, connecting with Gilly's nose. Black, warm ooze mixed with red. Gilly laughed, wiping its bleeding nose with its forearm. "Wait, wait," Gilly said, stepping back. "Wait, wait," he said, holding up the complicated metal rods to Mencken. "We can wrestle in moments. I'll be right back."

Mencken watched hopelessly as Gilly ran off toward the battle. He screamed, trying to get the foursome's attention again, trying to warn them, trying to let them know that he had failed, but still, he couldn't break their focus. Struggling to his feet, he stumbled forward to the crest of the hill. The battle still raged before him. Bodies of the beasts were piled at the bottom of the hill, but the monsters continued to file from the pink circle.

Gilly arrived at the edge of the portal to the other world. Seemingly unfazed by the carnage below, the Sinciput counted off four paces from the gateway.

Mencken frantically searched the ground with his eyes. Small metal parts and cut wires were scattered through the grass: the remnants of Gilly's craft. A wave of nausea came over him. He choked it down, shaking his head back to the moment, forcing his mind to stay focused on the task at hand. There, in the mess of discarded things, was white packaging paper.

Like a flag bearer claiming conquered land, Gilly slammed one of the metal rods into the ground. Fiddling with a knob at its top, he began to extend it up, expanding the rod like a tent pole.

Mencken spread the packaging out with his foot, knelt down, and jammed his bloody forearm into the pile. The paper filled with his blood, sticking to his arm. Scrambling, he laid the back of his forearm on a stretch of wire. With his free hand, he bent the thin metal strands around his arm and connected the ends of the wire, twisting them together, tighter and tighter, until the packaging paper was locked onto his wound.

Gilly ran his hands up and down the rod. The metallic pole began to glow and drew the edge of the coral circle towards its tip.

Mencken glanced down to the battle on the field and saw Jose slip on the oily ooze gathering at his feet. The teen fell, rolling several yards away from the action. Mencken could tell the team was fading. Agnew's arms had lost their feisty energy and she labored with every swing. Chris was spending more time with each combatant, no longer able to end them with a single blow.

Rothman screamed, noticing Gilly for the first time.

To compensate for the loss of Jose, Agnew attempted to move closer to the portal and fill in the gap, but she slipped as well and almost caught a Mardock claw in the jaw. Mencken held his breath, thinking the formation would collapse, but Jose rose to his feet and scrambled to retake his position in the V. With Jose back in place, at Rothman's command, the foursome to surge forward, but the stream of combatants wouldn't allow them to gain a step.

The corners of the pink circle continued to stretch until they met the edge of Gilly's rod. Agnew screamed in horror as three beasts raced from the newly expanded portal

Rothman bellowed, "Hold the line!"

The third monster flanked Agnew on the left, attempting to push her down into Jose and collapse the formation. Agnew threw a cross to the monster farthest on the outside, connecting with its jaw, sending it to the ground. She stepped around it, expanding the V.

Jose sliced the ankles of a monster on Agnew's right, and then, as he moved into her spot, he ran his laser-like fist across its neck.

Agnew surged up the hill, delivering a powerful jab to an oncoming Mardock's chest, successfully falling the beast with a single blow, and then crushing its head with her left boot.

The fight resumed at a heightened pace, with the foursome having expanded their formation to meet the increased number of combatants streaming from the portal.

Gilly clapped with glee from behind the magical entrance, jumping up and down to celebrate its success. The small creature turned and picked up the second rod where it lay in the grass. Lining up with the first rod, he began to count off four paces, clearly planning to expand the portal again, but as Gilly took his second step Mencken threw all his force into the beast. Like a linebacker taking down a quarterback from the blind side, he leveled the small creature with his right shoulder.

Gilly collided with the glowing rod planted in the ground. It sparked, and then went dark. The pink portal snapped back to its original size. Gilly screamed with rage. Striding toward the fallen Mencken, the short monster yelled, "Now! You makes me kill you now!"

Mencken lay on his stomach, his bleeding left arm pulled close to his body. He waited until the Sinciput got closer. He could hear it approaching. He visualized the monster's steps. He knew that he had to time his next move perfectly. Gilly was too fast and too strong for him to face off with directly. Surprise was his only weapon. If he waited too long, the beast would be on him, tearing his flesh from his bones with its shark like teeth. If he struck too early, Gilly would dodge and take his life in seconds.

Gilly continued to rant as he closed on Menkcen. "You dares to touch Gilly the Great, Gilly the Glorious. You dares to interfere. Now you dies. Now, not later. Now." The Sinciput was so close to its prey, its mouth had begun to water. Mencken could feel its excitement, its longing to see his blood spilt.

"Gilly will rip you's face off. Gilly rips you's face off with my bare hands," the monster said slowly, in order to savor the final moments before it pounced.

Mencken lay perfectly still in the grass, pretending to be

spent, listening to Gilly's approaching steps.

Gilly stopped above Mencken. The beast leaned in to grab the fallen reporter. A thousand methods of torture danced in its wild eyes.

"Now," Mencken said to himself. Pushing off with his bad shoulder, Mencken thrust his right hand forward with all his might. The discarded steel shard he'd been clutching stabbed Gilly in the chest.

Black blood spewed from the fresh wound. Taking a step back and clutching its shoulder, the monster let loose a high pitch shriek of surprise.

Mencken jumped to his feet. Letting go of the shard in the monster's chest, he dug into his pocket for his lighter. He flipped it open and sparked it with his thumb. A small orange and blue flame emerged.

Gilly's eyes grew wide with fear as the monster realized what was about to happen. He stepped backward again, preparing to turn and run, but his foot snagged a fallen piece of his construction, causing him to stumble. Catching himself with his left hand, he regained his feet, but before he could step, Mencken was on him.

Grabbing the metal that protruded from the center of the tiny monster with one hand, Mencken pulled the shard out of Gilly's chest and thrust the lighter forward, holding it to the fresh wound. "Burn you little bastard," Mencken whispered into the monster's ear.

Gilly hollowed in pain as his wound caught fire. The flame raced from the exterior of his body to the interior. His entire being filled with agony as the interior maze of his cardiovascular system was set ablaze.

Seeing the fire, Rothman screamed from behind Mencken, "RETREAT! EVERYONE! RETREAT!"

"Mencken, NO!" Chris yelled.

"Fuck!" Agnew screamed.

Holding the limp beast tight in a headlock with his good forearm, Mencken ran toward the entrance of the portal dragging Gilly along behind him. He had no idea what effect a blazing Gilly would have on the opening, but he figured it would be a show-stopper. The monster was heating up like a stovetop set to "High." Mencken's arm and chest began to blister from the heat of Gilly.

A Mardock, fresh from the portal, attempted to step in Mencken's path, but to Mencken and the muscle-bound beast's shock, the monster collapsed to its knees. A blue streak ran across the monster's neck, sending the monster's head falling to the right as its body fell forward at the feet of Jose.

Mencken came to a halt at the site of the decapitation. Vomit filled his mouth. He stumbled and let go of Gilly.

Jose grabbed the tiny beast by the neck and pivoted his hip, throwing Gilly's body into the mouth of the pink circle at the feet of two confused Mardocks who only just entered the fight. Completing his three-hundred-and-sixty degree spin, Jose pushed Mencken hard, launching both of them up the hill, to the back side of the portal.

Gilly's body hit the ground and ruptured. Liquid fire burst from his extremities and orifices, pouring onto the black-blood soaked hill. As the fire bomb that was once Gilly touched the grass, the hill sparked into a blaze, every drop of the black ooze igniting in bright blue flame.

Jose continued to shove Mencken, pushing him from the path of the growing fire. Once across the brick path, they fell onto their chests in the grass. The heat of the fire behind them licked their legs and backs.

Trying to catch his breath, Jose said, "We try not to do that shit until we can control it. You know, to avoid burning to death."

Mencken sat up, looked at Jose, and realized that the teen's face, shirt, and pants, were all thickly smeared with the black, flammable blood. "Oh, shit," Mencken said, suddenly realizing that he might have also ignited one of the foursome. "Sorry. I didn't-"

Jose smile. "It's fine. You're so slow, we were all able to get clear."

The two friends turned over to look at the blaze they had barely escaped. The entire hill was engulfed in seven-foot flames. Tiny orange embers danced in the evening sky, playing off the red sunset. The small burning particles drifted into the air, taking with them the evidence of what had just occurred. The pink circle flickered and then disappeared, vanishing into the orange, burning glow of the fire.

"At least we don't have to clean all that up," Chris said, sitting down on the other side of Mencken. He too was covered in the black oil.

"Yeah, especially since someone made us burn my truck," Agnew said, taking a seat next to Jose.

Chris put his arm around Mencken. "Next time, a little warning before you set the world on fire would be nice."

Distant sirens rang down the street, bouncing between nearby rowhomes, warning of the arrival of the Baltimore Fire Department. "Time to go," Chris said, standing. Reaching down, he offered Mencken a hand.

CHAPTER TWENTY-SIX

Imani's place felt warmer and more comfortable than before. A Bill Withers' song played softly through the house speakers. Imani, Chris, Agnew, and Mencken were spread out in a small circle around tables in the middle of the restaurant. Wanting to be ready for the returning heroes, Imani had closed early, throwing all her patrons out for the night. She had dinner waiting for them: warm tomato soup, grilled cheese sandwiches, and beer.

Chris and Agnew's laughter bounced through the empty space, overpowering the music, as Jose re-enacted the battle scene.

"And then Rothman was like…" With slow and exaggerate movements, the teen mocked Rothman's powerful moves, pretending to wield two giant sticks. "But then Agnew was all…" he continued, switching rapidly to a boxer's stance. Shadow boxing, he pretended to spar with an invisible opponent.

Imani laughed and took a sip of her beer. Chris drained his own glass, put his arm around her, and kissed her cheek. She tilted her head toward him, resting it on his shoulder. The scene gave Mencken a sense of warmth. A large, powerful smile broke out on his face, charging his whole body with a feeling of belonging. He sighed, and his eyes grew heavy.

"Do Mencken again," Agnew said. "Do Mencken."

Jose pretended to receive a punch to the face, falling backward to the ground with a loud crash. Agnew roared with laughter. "And then Imani," Agnew said. "He gets the bright idea to take his lighter out."

"Seven feet high," Jose said, standing up again. "Flames. Went. Seven. Feet. High. I bet grass doesn't grow on Federal Hill for another year."

Mencken stood, collecting his, Chris, and Imani's glasses. He placed them all on a small, black tray. "You want another?" he said to Agnew.

"Yeah, Fireball," she replied with a grin, passing him her glass.

Mencken smiled at the new nickname.

"Give me some of the thick stuff," Agnew said.

Mencken added her glass to the other three. Gingerly, he slid the tray off the table with his good hand. Balancing it as best he could, he made his way to the bar behind them.

"Why don't you do Chris?" Imani said.

"Because he can't," Chris teased.

Laughter rose behind Mencken as Jose attempted a Chris imitation.

Stepping behind the bar, Mencken placed the tray carefully on the countertop. He looked at the taps. There were seven options. He had no idea what most of them were. The stylized pulls and bright label colors did nothing to indicate which of the options would be heavy enough to satisfy Agnew.

"I find the one second to the left to be the most satisfying," a deep voice said quietly.

The rumble caught Mencken off guard. He jump with surprise, turning to see Rothman sitting in shadows at the end of the bar. Mencken stepped down and grabbed the giant man's glass. Pulling forward on the suggested tap, he filled the glass with a dark drown brew. He then passed the full, heavy glass back to Rothman.

"Thank you," Rothman said.

Mencken filled Chris, Imani, and Agnew's glasses from the same tap. With the glasses full, he turned and placed them on the bar behind him. Jose was still acting out battle scenes. He looked at the small family and smiled again.

"It's impossible without it," Rothman said warmly, also admiring the scene.

"What is?" Mencken said, curiously.

"Battling monsters," Rothman said. "It's impossible without a family to come home to. This moment is what makes the battle survivable. Without it, one would lose heart in the heat of the battle. When the world is on fire, we need this to sustain us. We need the knowledge of this to beckon us home."

Mencken smiled for a third time. "Yeah," he said, knowing exactly what he needed to do. A surge of energy filled his legs, as an unexpected urgency overcame him. "Hey," he said to Rothman. "Deliver these for me." Mencken pushed the tray of full glasses toward the giant. Without waiting for an answer, Mencken stepped around the bar and headed toward the front door.

"Best of luck," Rothman called with a laugh.

The chill of the night air bit at his nose. His heart throbbed with anticipation. He crossed the street without looking, believing that not even a speeding car could slow him now. He threw open the door to his building and strode across the threshold. He took the stairs two at a time, not wanting to waste the extra second it would take to step on each one.

It was only there, in front of her door, that he slowed. What would he say? What if he was wrong? What if she didn't return his affection? Filled with fear, he stopped. Staring at her door, he questioned himself. He questioned whether this was the right course of action. Maybe he should come back tomorrow with roses, or maybe he should have chocolates, or maybe he should write her a love letter? He was a writer after all. Isn't that how he should express himself to her for the first time? The fearful side of his soul gained a foothold. "A letter would work," he mumbled to himself. "I could just slide it under the door. Maybe not even sign it. That could be romantic."

He thought about the past month. He thought about Anita Dickson and the Clevelands. He remembered the glee in Gilly's eyes as the monster took his teeth. He remembered Jose on the City Hall lawn. He thought about the giant fire on the hill. The images washed over him, one after the other. So much had changed in the last few weeks. The world was a different place than it had been before, a place full of mysterious dangers, larger than he imagined. He thought about Imani taking Chris to the basement after the devastating loss, and then he remembered Chris kissing Imani on the cheek after the eventful victory. He heard Rothman's words again, "It's impossible without a family to come home to."

Courage boomed in his chest, supplied by the knowledge that tomorrow was uncertain, that he was not guaranteed another dawn, and that he needed a partner if he was to face the problems of the city. He needed someone who would kiss him on the cheek, someone he could take to the basement after a loss. He needed family. He needed love. He needed her. He wanted her. He knew he would fail without her. His mind made up, Mencken pounded on her door with his good hand.

And then, she was there. Her thick black hair pulled back into a ponytail. Her green eyes sparkling at him like Christmas lights on a tree. Her perfect lips drifted into a smile. Mencken looked her up and down. She was in a ratty, loose-fitting, gray t-shirt and old, thinning blue sweat pants. Mencken smiled at her fuzzy green slippers. She looked perfect. She was perfect.

"Hey," he said.

Rosie noticed his left arm. Imani had cleaned it,

wrapped it, and put it in a sling. "Are you alright?" Rosie said, reaching for him.

Mencken grabbed her hand before she could touch him. He held on to it, not wanting to lose her, afraid she might disappear. She looked at their hands, tangled together, and she smiled.

"I was wondering," Mencken said. "If you might want to, um." Words left him in the face of her beauty. "If you, um. Well," he stumbled. "If you might want to go get some dinner? Or maybe just some coffee? Or something?" He looked at his feet, embarrassed by his fumbling. He knew he was ruining the moment. He was certain he was losing her, all because he couldn't put a few sentences together.

Rosie squeezed his hand. She placed her free palm on his cheek. Pulling down gently, she guided his lips to meet hers. Relief and joy rushed through Mencken's veins as their mouths connected for the first time. She held him there for a moment, and then moved back. Grinning up at him, she said, "I thought you'd never ask."

EPILOUGE

Hunter couldn't help but smile when his boys took their positions. Quincy stood in the street with his back to the driver's side door; Kamal stationed himself at the front door to the hotel, watching the lobby; and Dominic, the leader of the three, opened rear passenger door. The three teens were focused, noticing every movement around them, preparing to intercept any potential threat.

Hunter stepped from the dark car into the sunlight. He looked into the sky, savoring the warmth on his face. "Has the building been cleared?" he asked his second in command.

"Yes, sir," Dominic said, scanning the street. The boy was tall and muscular with the shoulders of a linebacker. In his black suit and sunglasses, few would have guessed he was only sixteen.

"Has everyone arrived?" Hunter asked, looking his protégé in the eye.

"Everyone is present, sir. Five came with escorts. They've been disarmed and seated in the hotel bar."

"Excellent," Hunter said. "Let's take the boss inside."

Dominic moved toward the hotel door. In response, Kamal entered the lobby to secure the elevator. Hunter stepped forward to allow his boss to exit the black sedan.

In contrast to the four members of his security team, Ignatius Deceus was not dressed in a black suit. Mr. Deceus, or Iggy to his friends, was a short man in his mid-fifties. His thinning hair was streaked with gray, and the corners of his eyes were marked with smile lines. He was dressed comfortably in khakis, a pale blue Oxford shirt, and navy blue sweater. Although he'd lived in Baltimore for more than two decades, his accent still gave him away as a native of the Deep South. "Is everything set?" he asked Hunter as he stepped from the car to the sidewalk.

"Yes, sir, Mr. Deceus," Hunter replied.

"Excellent," Deceus said.

Hunter led the way for Deceus into the building. Quincy, the small, quick, fourteen-year-old member of Hunter's team brought up the rear. No one bothered them as they walked through the ornate lobby. Few of the staff knew that Deceus owned the building. In their eyes, he was simply another VIP on his way to a meeting in the penthouse conference room.

Dominic was waiting at the elevator for them, holding the door open for them. Hunter and Deceus entered first, then Dominic and Quincy.

"Do you have the video ready?" Deceus asked.

"Everything is ready," Hunter replied.

"Getting that footage was excellent work," Deceus said. "Excellent work."

"The boys did well, sir," Hunter said.

Dominic and Quincy showed no sign they could hear the conversation.

"It's a game changer," Deceus said. "A real game changer. We might just pull this whole thing off after all."

"I have no doubt, sir," Hunter said.

The elevator came to a halt on the twenty-second floor, and the door slid open. Kamal, a lean thirteen-year-old with a scar above his right eye, stood at attention in the hall. The four new arrivals stepped off the elevator.

"Boys," Hunter said. "Secure the room."

Without a word, led by Dominic, the three teens moved down the hall and through the two large double doors at the far end.

"You know," Deceus said, checking his teeth in the golden framed hallway mirror. "When you first told me your plan for those little monsters, I was skeptical, but you've really worked them into a fine team."

"Thank you, sir," Hunter said, standing behind his boss.

"But still, I worry," Deceus said as he pulled the cuffs of his shirt out from under his sweater. "You need to be more careful with them. All this social media nonsense they've been up to. It's going to get them caught."

"We have it under control, sir."

"That's the thing about monsters," Deceus said. He combed his eyebrows with his thumb, making sure all the hairs were in line. "You're never really in control."

"Not that long ago, I thought all rich white men were monsters. Labels are a matter of perspective," Hunter said with a smile.

Deceus turned to face the man he thought of as a son. He squeezed his right shoulder affectionately and smiled. "You've got me there," he said. Then he turned and walked toward the conference room. Hunter followed behind.

The conference room was dominated by a large, round, mahogany table. Around the table were eleven brown leather chairs. Two walls of the room were glass, giving a stunning view of the city. A large flat screen television was mounted on the third wall. Three waiters dressed in white buzzed around the room clearing breakfast plates from the table and refilling coffee cups.

Everyone on the council was in their usual seats. Sam Dandrip, the local media celebrity, sat at the chair closest to the door. Samson Black, the City Council President, nursed a brandy across from him. The four real-estate moguls, John Hammerjam, Sarah Atkinson, Rufus Gilford, and Hoon Gahn laughed together quietly to right. Police Commissioner Eddy and Ronaldo Glass, the CEO of Baltimore City Schools, chatted casually with the gangster known as Agamemnon. To the left of Sam was Hannibal Dula, an aging, dignified gangster who controlled the Baltimore docks and much of the east side of the city. Hannibal quietly reviewed email on his cell phone. It was a dignified group of local titans. Knowing they had all come because they revered and served his mentor made Hunter smile.

Hunter's boys stood at attention in three corners of the room. Hunter had trained them well. He knew that with a snap of his fingers, the teens would kill the ten council members without hesitation. The council members knew it too, which explained the occasional nervous glances they gave the teens.

Deceus' entrance told the wait staff that their jobs were finished for the morning. They rapidly wrapped up their tasks and exited the room through the doors behind Hunter.

"Sam," Deceus said, affectionately squeezing Sam's shoulder with one hand while extending his other for a shake.

"Iggy," Sam said. He stood out of respect, and shook Iggy's hand.

This was Deceus' custom. At every meeting he shook hands, smiled, and exchanged laughs with each person at the table. Hunter, in contrast, waited stoically behind his boss, occasionally offering a nod of welcome, but never sharing a pleasantry.

"Sit, sit," Deceus said to Sam. "How's that new horse? An American Saddlebred? Is that right? Have you had much time to ride recently?"

"Not nearly enough," Sam said. "She just arrived last week. Got her from a stable in Alexandria. I'm excited about getting her out and about though. You should come and join me. It would be an honor to have you and your daughter out to the farm again. I'll give you the first ride. Maybe for dinner next week?"

"Well, I can't speak for Abigail, but I would love to come out. But only if you promise to make that incredible manicotti. I'm telling you Sam, that pasta was a work of art."

"Absolutely," Sam said enthusiastically.

"I'll have my secretary call and set a date then," Deceus said. He squeezed Sam's shoulder again, gave Sam an affectionate smile, and then moved on to the next member at the table.

Hunter respected that his boss knew every detail of each council member's life: their hobbies, their habits, and their vices. He'd paid good money to have each of them watched and profiled. While the council members saw of Deceus as a friend, Hunter knew Deceus saw them as pieces on his chess board. Deceus moved them around however he wished.

Once the round had been made, Deceus took his seat at the table. Hunter stood behind him, taking the same stance as his boys in the corners.

"Thank y'all for coming this morning," Deceus said. "I apologize that I couldn't join you for breakfast. I assume the food was to your liking."

There were nods and grateful affirmations from around the table.

"I know how busy y'all are," Deceus continued. "And I can't tell y'all how grateful I am that you prioritize these monthly gatherings. There are three things on this morning's agenda. We need to discuss next steps for the Pimlico development, Mr. Gahn has proposed an innovative solution to our North Avenue predicament, and Councilman Black will provide us with an update on the upcoming Mayoral race. But before we launch into those items of business, there is something of interest I would like to bring to y'all's attention."

Hunter reached forward, retrieved a small black remote from the table and pointed it at the large television on the wall. The screen came to life with a video of Federal Hill. At the top of the hill was a large pink circle. There appeared to be giant, muscular people streaming from it, entering into a fist-fight with four other people on the hill.

The members of the council were enraptured by the events on the screen. They'd never seen anything like it. Sam was the first to speak. "Was this movie made recently?" he blurted out. "The CGI is incredible. Is this a Baltimore-based production company?"

Deceus laughed. "Sam, you know, I thought the same thing when Hunter showed it to me last night. But this isn't a movie. This video was captured by one of Hunter's boys yesterday, just before sunset. This is real, Gentlemen. It's all real."

The room sat in stunned silence.

"Hunter, would you mind explaining further? You know the details far better than I do."

Hunter hesitated, watching the video. When the screen zoomed in on the pink circle at the top of the hill, Hunter paused the movie. "My boys have been following a blogger we've been toying with recently."

"Quite an ambitious young man," Deceus interjected. "Maybe a future candidate for this table."

"In the past few days the blogger had taken to following these four on the hill. We didn't think much of it at first. It seemed to be a potential story he was chasing, but then yesterday there was an engagement on the lawn of City Hall, and then this appeared at the top of Federal Hill. As you can see," Hunter said, motioning toward the television screen with the remote. "It appears this pink circle is a doorway of some kind, and that there is a large mass of men on the other side."

"Y'all know what I see here?" Deceus said with a smile. "I see opportunity. Commissioner Eddy, you and I have discussed before how a private security force might have a positive impact on the city, relieving your officers from some of their more physical burdens. And Hannibal and Agamemnon, imagine no longer having to struggle to raise up street thugs to manage y'all's affairs. What if I could equip y'all with a hundred of those beasts? Can you imagine?" Deceus smacked the table with excitement. "Now I don't know who they are, or where that pink door leads, but I'm going to find out. I'm going to find out, and I promise y'all, we will harness that force. We'll harness it, and wield it to accomplish our agenda. This gentlemen," Deceus said pointing at the screen. "This is the future army we need."

TO BE CONTINUED

For a free novella from the Defense of Reality series, visit
www.VagrantMisunderstandings.com

COMING DECEMBER 2016

40635688R00125

Made in the USA
Middletown, DE
18 February 2017